THE GLASS PEDESTAL

By

Silvia I. Petretti

FM Publishing Company
Casa Grande, Arizona 85130

The Glass Pedestal

Published by:

FM Publishing Company
P.O. Box 10744
Casa Grande, AZ 85130
www.fasthelpministries.com
fmpublishing@cox.net

The Glass Pedestal

Printed in the United States of America

ISBN 9781931671200

Library of Congress Control Number 2010938293

Dedication

These Stories are about my family and are dedicated to my parents and grandparents, who gave me love and direction and from whom I inherited their God given talents and style. They are with their Heavenly Father now but do visit me now and then in my dreams. I know I will be reunited with them in Heaven at the end of my time here on Gods' Earth.

PART I

1942

NEW BEGINNINGS

Chapter 1

It was a lovely, sunny day, not rare for December in southern California. It was a perfect 78 degrees, not a cloud in the sky, a slight breeze just enough to ruffle and slightly lift one's skirt, a wonderful day for a stroll down Hollywood Boulevard. It was noontime and the street was crowded with busy holiday shoppers and lunchtime escapees. Mary had left her job and began her stroll with anticipation; she wanted to be on the other side of the counter to enjoy the holiday spirit and the beautiful day with the excited people she had been encountering all day.

Mary enjoyed waiting on the customers this time of year; everyone buying presents and asking her advice on what a woman would want for Christmas. She was a sales clerk at the accessories and cosmetics counter at J. C. Penney, she had found her job easy enough, as the stores had been taking on extra help for the holiday season. Mary was not in a hurry. She was enjoying the day, she had feelings inside of such contentment, that she had to contain herself so as not to wear a big grin. She would stop and gaze in the windows at the festive Christmas decorations, Jolly Santa's with big white beards and bright red suits, little Elves and Reindeer. She especially liked the nativity scenes, the little baby in the basket with Mary and Joseph gazing with wonder at the child.

Mary was brought up in the strict atmosphere of the Southern Baptist Church, and was named Mary, after Jesus' Mother. Mary always thought this was a name that was hard to live up to, as Ada; her mother had always reminded her whenever Mary did something that displeased Ada. "Now Mary," she would say, "don't forget, you know you were named after Jesus' mother." Of course, Mary's mother didn't say this very often because Mary had a sweet disposition and charming personality, and loved her mother with great passion, as Ada loved Mary the same way.

Mary had arrived in Los Angeles only a few weeks before. She had caught a bus to Hollywood and had walked the streets with her one carpet bag in hand until she saw an inviting home with a sign that said, ROOM FOR RENT. The room she was to rent was small and the furniture was sparse, but it was light and airy with fluffy curtains and she could open the windows and let the breezes in to gently flap the curtains. The landlady discovered that Mary did not have a job, but Mary was not a person to be denied, with her sweet face and decent clothes. Mrs. Rafferty could not resist her. Mrs. Rafferty reminded Mary of her mother, and each was willing to take a chance on the other. All Mary had brought with her was a few pretty dresses she knew she would need on a new job.

She had been planning this adventure to California for a couple of years. She had to get out of the little west Texas town she was from. It had been hard to leave her mother and her brother, CL, but her life had come to a dead end. To escape, she had joined the circus. With her first paycheck from J.C. Penny, she had bobbed her light brown hair and bleached it a creamy blonde like the starlets whose pictures she had always admired. She bought a couple of potted flowering plants for the little room, and to go over the foldout sofa, she bought a pretty print of a field of pastel colored flowers. Being from West Texas where it was hard to grow anything but oil, Ada always worked hard and long in the garden and her flowers were always enjoyed by all her neighbors. Mary needed these touches to remind her of home.

On this day, on this stroll, Mary was wearing one of her favorite dresses: a striking print in a silky fabric with peach colored flowers on a black background. It had a white collar, and on the long fitted sleeves, white cuffs. She wore peach-hued lipstick, and her hair shined with bright sparkles from the previous night's vigorous washing. The sunlight bounced off each strand. She stopped to gaze at the holiday dress that had caught her eye in the department store window; it was red velvet with old antique lace trimming the v-neck and the sleeves to the plastic knuckles of the mannequin. She noticed her reflection in the window; her hair created a halo around her head, the sun shining through it. She thought 'Boy that's some hair, well alright, I do look good.' The grin she had been suppressing now escaped and she almost giggled.

"You know, I think you would look wonderful in that dress."

The deep voice behind her startled her out of her daydream. She turned around abruptly and her elbow hit the man standing behind her right in the solar plexus. He let out a gasp and started laughing.

"I'm sorry; I didn't mean to startle you," he said a little breathlessly.

"No please, I'm sorry," said Mary, a bit embarrassed. "Did I hurt you?"

"No, it's my fault, I couldn't resist, and you looked so lost in thought."

Mary looked at him and smiled. "I was imagining myself in that dress. It appears you were reading my mind."

The man admired Mary's deep blue eyes, fringed with dark lashes that curled delicately, nearly to her expressive brows. Mary smiled and her already rosy cheeks resembled two beautiful apples. She had a small dimple that divided her chin ever so lightly. The man had been watching her and slowly following her since the first time he spotted her as he left his office building heading for his lunch break. He estimated Mary to be about 20 years old. He decided he liked the way her curls perfectly framed her oval face, her flawless ivory skin and especially the way the silky material of her dress clung appealingly to her gentle curves.

He was still staring at her when she lowered her eyes as her face flushed slightly from embarrassment; he, too, was smiling.

"I must confess I have been following you for a couple of blocks. You are irresistible, you know." He paused noticing she was blushing, "Please don't be embarrassed. . ." He fidgeted. "I have gone about this all wrong. Are you hungry? Can I make this up to you by buying you lunch? There is a little café I enjoy just down the street."

Mary was wary of men in a big city, being single wasn't easy and he had admitted he was following her. "Well, I am hungry, I was going to grab a sandwich at

Woolworth's, but go to lunch with you, and I don't even know you."

"Well," he said, "You could say I know you already, I read your mind, didn't I?" Her laugh was a cheerful tingling sound to him. He waited.

"Ok, it's just lunch, you seem harmless enough. Tell me your name and then I won't feel so strange."

"My name is Dante Vianney, what's yours?"

"Hmmmmm, that's Italian, isn't it, are you from back east? Is that a Brooklyn accent I detect?"

"I'm afraid so, I am from New York, I grew up in Brooklyn, and all of my family is still in Yonkers New York."

"My name is Mary, Mary Eden."

"Mary Eden is a nice name for a lovely girl, are you from around here?"

"No I have just arrived here a few weeks back." "Where are you from?" He had noticed her southern accent, not slow and syrupy like the Deep South, but slow and sexy.

"I'm from a small town in west Texas originally, but I have been all over the country this past year." She answered happily, smiling then frowning, bewildered at herself as to why she was giving this stranger so much information about herself.

"Well, Mary. . ." He was watching her, amused at her quick change of expressions, "It sounds like you have had an interesting year, I would be happy to hear more over lunch."

As they started off down the street, Mary said a silent prayer, 'Please God if you still love me, let this be right, it seems right.' Mary felt she didn't deserve God's love anymore, she still believed he was there but her prayers were not as strong as they had been. She had sinned in her eyes and was ashamed of what had happened to her. She often cried at night with shame, but in the morning she was able to thank Jesus for the day and to push aside her inner torment. She was living is a state of un-grace in her mind, not satisfied, and, as many young people who have left home and are looking for their independence, also looking for answers that would justify their departure from family and the religious values so instilled in them by their mothers.

He placed his hand on her waist. She sent him a quick look of protest to his touch of familiarity. He noticed but did not remove his hand. He led her down the street toward the little café he had in mind. They walked along in silence, he leading and she being led, past the store windows shimmering with reflections of each of them. The bright noonday sunlight warmed them to where little dew drops of perspiration appeared on their foreheads and noses.

Mary reached into her pocketbook, removed a handkerchief, and dabbed it gently around her face. She looked up at him at the moment he was reaching for his handkerchief to do the same. "Can you believe its December and almost Christmas?" she asked him. "I know that's Southern California for you. Back home it would be snowing and we would be slipping on the sidewalk ice and wearing big heavy coats, instead of dabbing sweat from our brows."

He didn't respond. He replaced his handkerchief in the breast pocket of his of his dark gray suit jacket. Walking on the right street side of Mary with his left hand on her waist, he was able to accomplish the feat of cleaning his brow and replacing the handkerchief without removing his hand from her waist.

He noticed the slightness of her body. They continued on in renewed silence the click, click, click of her high heels on the sidewalk being the only sound they heard, and the hustle and bustle of the busy shoppers going unnoticed. She could hardly breathe; his hand on her waist felt wonderful, but she wished he would take it away so she could breathe. Suddenly, he removed his hand, again, as if reading her mind, and she sighed.

They arrived at the café; it was charming. They were greeted by a small thin cheerful waiter wearing a large white apron that covered him from just under his chin to halfway between his knees and ankles. He wore a small black bowtie and had a thin black mustache. His black-dyed looking hair was slicked across the top of his almost bald head. His small black eyes glistened and squinted when he smiled at them. They told him there were only two of them and could they be seated on the patio. The waiter led through the colorful café past other diners seated round white wrought tables, with potted Geraniums of all colors all around. They passed through French doors to the patio which seemed so much like a garden with just a few tables place under arbors of vines and flowers.

"This is just beautiful." Mary exclaimed.

"I thought you would like it." Dante smiled at her.

They ordered sandwiches and talked again of the weather. Mary tried to eat but she spent most of the time taking in the sight of him. He was tall, probably six feet, and you couldn't miss the perfect white teeth when he smiled. In fact, he seemed to be smiling all the time. She noticed a dimple in his left cheek, his dark wavy hair combed back from his forehead, a lock falling to one side over his forehead, giving him a rakish look. He had dark brown eyes, devil eyes, Ada would say. She said all men with brown eyes had devil eyes. His were soft and sleepy, bedroom eyes, Mary thought. What would her mother think if she saw him? She glanced up at the big clock on the wall.

"Oh dear, look what time it is! I have to get back to work, I can't be late, I just got this job." She started to get up from the table dropped her napkin on the floor and hurried to pick it up and started to leave.

"OK, Ok, I don't want to be the downfall of my new friend," Dante told her. He paid the bill and led her to the street. She broke away and started off by herself.

"Wait, wait a minute, please," he called out to her.

"I have to go," she said. "But thanks for lunch."

"It was my pleasure, but please, how will I get in touch with you again?"

She had turned and was walking half backwards, in a hurry, but she wanted to answer him. "I work at J. C. Penny, at the cosmetic counter, see you."

She arrived out of breath one minute before one o'clock. Her supervisor, Beth, a young attractive woman close to Mary's age, had long black hair and almond shaped eyes, was busy with a customer displaying the various shades of red lipstick, scraping off a bit with a toothpick and applying it to the back of the customer's elegant hand.

"This shade would look good on you," said Beth. "It tends more to the coral shade that will complement our peachy complexion and your reddish hair."

"I think you are right." The customer paused. "You know, I was looking at a dress this shade in the dress department, I think I will take the lipstick you recommended and I just might buy the dress too.

"What's the name of the lipstick?"

"It's Seductive Siren." Beth smiled wickedly.

"Very interesting, it sounds like fun, I can hardly wait to try it out."

"Treat yourself to the dress too, it's Christmas after all."

Mary had been watching Beth with awe. Beth was good and she was also right about the lipstick. Beth took a small sheet of green tissue paper, wrapped the lipstick, put it in a small holiday bag and completed the transaction. She thanked the customer with greetings of "Happy Holidays" and then turned to Mary.

"Well, you sure cut it close today, you are usually early. What kept you?"

"Today was special."

"How so?" Beth asked.

Mary turned her head and looked down at the counter and scarves she was arranging, as if embarrassed. "Well I met a very handsome man and he took me to lunch."

"Oh really, only a few weeks in town and you are already in love."

Mary laughed. "Well not exactly. I only just met him, but he seemed nice and he seemed to like me."

"Who wouldn't? Tell me about him."

"There's not much to tell, you can't learn a lot on a lunch hour, but he's handsome and he smiles a lot."

"Be careful, there are a lot of jerks in this town."

"Don't worry, I'll be careful, I am not about to take chances anymore." She was remembering her last encounter with a man she mistakenly trusted.

Just then a customer wandered over to the counter. Smiling Mary began to help her.

"I'm going now," said Beth, "Maybe I'll meet a handsome stranger on *my* lunch break." she laughed again as she left.

Chapter 2

Mary decided to walk home after work. It was still warm and although she was tired she wanted the exercise since the weather was bound to turn cold soon. California was strange, the weather would be cold and rainy one day and wonderfully warm and sunny the next. And the palm trees everywhere; it was neat. The people were very different from the country people she had known all her life, some of them were scary, and some very friendly. Back home everybody was kind and friendly. She was lucky to have met Beth; she was great, and they became friends fast. Beth was a dancer and wanted to get into show business. Mary wasn't interested; she was just looking for some peace in her life. She had thought she wanted show business when she joined the circus, but her taste for it had now turned sour. For a young woman it seemed she had been through a lot.

A dog barked and startled her out of her reveries; it was a small poodle in a fenced yard with a high shrill, yap, yap, yap. Two boys passed her on bicycles, one chubby with his tummy hanging over his belt, the other, thin with sandy colored hair, reminding her of Little Dewey. 'I missed home, Little Dewey and Mother.' she thought.

It was getting chilly, the sun had just set, a few clouds had formed late in the afternoon and now reflected the sun in many shades of brilliant oranges and pinks. She thought of the many sunsets she had watched in the big West Texas sky, while sitting on the back porch of her home in the old swing with Ada and sipping cool glasses of sweet tea, then Ada going into the kitchen to prepare dinner and her going to help her, and the rays of the sun sneaking through the wavy glass windows then leaving the room slowly and having to turn on the lamp to finish. She thought again of how much she missed her home and tears came to her eyes. Little Dewey, I can't call him that anymore, he likes CL, he is almost 18 years old, how he got his name CL was probably from Ada calling him Dewey Cecil whenever he was in trouble, and the Cecil coming out like CCCLLLLLLLLL. I'll write them as soon as I get home, I'll tell Ada about Dante, oh no, those dark brown eyes, maybe not, I'll wait till another time.

Ada was a wonderful woman, always trying to make things right through all kinds of misery, she was all Southern Baptist and praying all the time, every night on her knees at the bedside, no matter what was going on. She went around the house singing church songs like

Rock of Ages and *When the Roll is called up yonder*, whenever Dewey Sr. was out and it was just her and the kids. If he was there and she absently started singing, he would say, "Stop that loony church singing, I hear it enough on Sunday Mornings and all through the week when I pass the church, come on woman give me some peace."

Ada was born in Mississippi as were Mary and CL, but had left a few years back with a couple of her brothers to live in West Texas where they could get work in the oil fields. Ada had never been anywhere but the South, and she still had the attitude of the South inbred in her. People of dark or black shin were either foreigners or coloreds and she had a fear of people of color. She was always kind but still wary, therefore dark brown or black eyes were devil eyes to her.

Mary arrived at the small gate in front of the house where she had her room, opened the gate and walked up the sidewalk between two small patches of lawn to the large columned porch; she stopped to admire the flowers in the flower garden in front of the porch. They were what had first attracted her to the house. It reminded her of home. Ada always had beautiful flowers. She supplied the flowers for the Sunday Morning Church Service every week. She skipped up the steps and stopped to get her mail from the little blue mailbox with her name on it. "Oh, great, a letter from home; maybe now I can stop being so lonely." she said to herself "I'll brew a cup of tea and read the letter while I have some of my tea."

She fumbled in her pocketbook until she found her keys, opened the door and flipped on the lamp. She removed her high heels, sat on the sofa, put Ada's letter on the coffee table, and began to rub her feet, they were sore, and she was more tired than she thought. The letter and the tea forgotten, she decided to rest for a minute and pulled her afghan, a present from Ada she cherished because Ada had made it herself, 'this afghan has been everywhere with me,' she thought as she drifted off into a deep sleep.

She felt a feather light touch on her cheek, she awoke and realized it was morning and she had been dreaming about Dante and in her dream he had just gently kissed her cheek. 'How silly of me,' she thought. 'I'll probably never see him again.' She glanced at the little clock on the side table and realized it was 7 a.m. and time to get up. She noticed Ada's letter on the table and decided she would read it while she had the cup of tea she had planned to have last night. As she was making the tea she admired the little tea set she had purchased at the Salvation Army; it was very delicate and pretty and had cost very little. She had always enjoyed a cup of tea in the mornings with Ada. She opened Ada's letter in anticipation, letters from home always a comfort to her.

It began as all Ada's letters did;

Dearest Mary, I miss you so much, I hope you are doing well in your new life. I have important news. Since you left things here at home have gotten worse. Your father has been drinking most of the time now. And CL and I can't take it anymore. He takes everything out on CL; he abuses him so much when he is drinking. CL has joined the Navy; I hated it so, but I had to give my permission because we had no other choice. I was afraid your Daddy would really hurt him bad next time.

By the time you get this letter he will be gone. I am at Uncle Henry's. I don't know what I will do; I am all right here for awhile. I can't go back, I packed what I could in the trunk and Uncle Henry came and got me after your Daddy left to go drinking again. You know I don't have much left since the fire so I got most of the important stuff in the trunk.

I don't think he knew I was gone until the next day. He came over here to Henry's, still drunk, and tried to get into it with Uncle Henry and we had to call the Sheriff.

Please don't worry about me, I have a little money saved I hid from your Daddy just in case. I will let you know when I decide what to do. Be careful please, for my sake, I hated you leaving, but now, I see it was probably for the best considering all that has gone on now.

All my love and God bless you and keep you. You're, missing you Mother.

'Of course I will worry,' thought Mary. She had been crying since the part about CL going to the Navy, the tears kept dropping on the pages as she read the letter. 'Little Dewey in the Navy, and a war going on, why he was just a kid.' She knew what home life was when Dewey Sr. was drinking and CL had been the one to get the most abuse. 'And Mama leaving, oh God how will I get through this day, Oh God please watch over CL and Mama, don't let anything happen to them, I know I have done things wrong but don't let them suffer for what I have done. Please God don't let this be my punishment.'

She managed to get to work and Beth noticed right away there was something wrong. When Beth asked her, Mary said, "I can't talk about it right now; I will tell you later when I feel better. Ok."

"Ok, I'll be here all day," Beth assured her.

The day passed and Mary thanked God it was so busy she hardly had time for thoughts. That night she wrote a letter to Ada and asked for CL's address; Mary told Ada she would try and send some money to her from her next paycheck. She wanted to help but she knew in the next letter from Ada she would refuse the money. 'At least I can write to CL' she thought, and then she started crying and got on her knees and prayed out loud to God.

"Please God, Please God, watch over him. He is so sweet, so beautiful, so unlike Daddy, he never deserved what Daddy did to him. You made him perfect, maybe too perfect and that's why Daddy picked on him so much. He was probably jealous of the attention and love me and Mama showered on him. But God, we couldn't help it. Oh why was I so stupid to think only of myself and leave them alone? Forgive me God, I have sinned terribly and I want you with me and CL and Mama now, please forgive me."

She couldn't go on she was crying hysterically but she felt, in her heart, that God had heard her this time, and knew if she believed he forgave her maybe she could forgive herself. She then whimpered into a restless sleep.

Mary was still tired when she woke the next morning, but even though she felt some peace from her prayers the night before, she was still very upset and worried about her family. She got dressed for work, taking special care with the way she looked. She put on a pretty navy blue dress, trimmed in white, and navy and white spectator pumps. She fluffed up her hair, applied a little rough, and a tender red lipstick. It was cloudy and appeared to be threatening rain. So she took her camel-colored wool coat along with her umbrella. Maybe, she thought if I look good I will feel better. It was a just a few days until Christmas and this added to her loneliness.

Beth noticed that Mary seemed better and commented on the fact. Mary thanked her and explained about the letter and how it had upset her. Beth said she didn't blame her at all and that she hoped everything would work out all right. A little bit before noon Mary suggested Beth take her lunch early because she didn't feel like eating and just wanted to keep busy. Beth protested, saying that Mary needed to eat to keep up her strength. Mary resisted and said Beth could bring her back something to snack on. Beth finally agreed and left for lunch. After Beth left and it had slowed down a bit, Mary started to think about things again. She began rearranging the merchandise to keep her busy, but she felt close to tears again. She brought a pretty perfume bottle from under the counter to place on display. As she was putting it down, a large hand covered hers.

"Hello, Mary." She looked up into Dante's soft brown eyes.

"You look very pretty today, but I don't see that sparkle in your eyes I saw the other day." He had observed her briefly before he approached the counter and had noticed she was looking sad. A desire had overtaken him to make things right for her for the rest of her life. "Is there anything I can do for you, I came to ask you to go to lunch with me again, and maybe that will cheer you up?" He placed his other hand over hers and gazed into her eyes.

She removed her hand, the familiarity making her nervous, then she felt sorry, he was only trying to be kind to her. "Thank you for the offer it is very kind of you, but Beth has taken my lunch hour and I have to stay here today."

"Well then, how about dinner? I can't leave you like this, I think you could use some cheering up and I am a good listener."

"Okay, you're probably right, I will accept your invitation, and try to be good company." She smiled then and he noticed some of the sparkle come back into her eyes.

"Good, I can come for you after work then we could go back to the little café, you seemed to like it, and they have a great dinner menu." He said smiling brightly, as if he had won a great prize. Mary was beginning to feel better; his smile was infectious.

"That will be fine. I get off at five-thirty." Sounds good, I'll be here. I do hope you have a better afternoon."

"I'll try. Thanks. See you then."

The rest of the day was better. With the heartache from Ada's letter, she had almost forgotten about Dante, and seeing him again had lifted her spirits. Thank You Jesus, she thought.

Mary passed the day in eager anticipation of the evening ahead. She was glad she had worn the navy dress. It was made of good material and it would still look nice at the end of the day. Her clothes were not expensive but they were not cheap either. She had saved most of the money she had made in the circus and spent most of it on a new wardrobe. She knew she would soon be in L.A. and her simple country clothes would not do. So when the circus had gone to big cities, she had gone shopping in the more fashionable shops and bought a new dress and shoes in every big city.

She was lucky to get the job as an Elephant Rider right away in the circus. Most people had to work their way up. However, Ada was appalled and she didn't write to Mary for a month. "How can a good Baptist girl expose herself like that?" she had exclaimed when Mary had called her a few days after leaving with just a note left behind. "And you know Mary this is a party line and I am sure everyone will know about this by the end of the morning since those old church ladies sure do love to gossip. How am I going to hold my head up in church?"

"But mom," Mary had said, "I had to leave, you know that."

"No I don't, I don't understand at all. Leaving family and friends like that."

"The circus was just there and I knew if I didn't leave then, Daddy would have never let me go."

"And anyway I am not going to make a career out of the circus. It's only temporary. I would have never saved any money there, working at the soda shop."

"I don't care it's just awful the way you left. You broke my heart, getting up and just finding a note from you." Ada said, crying.

Mary said, "Mama, I am so sorry I didn't want to hurt anybody. It was very hard for me to leave you all, but I just had to. Please mama I need your support now."

"I don't know how I can do that the way I feel right now, but I love you, and I will be praying for you. Please be careful," Ada pleaded. She did start to return Mary's letters and try to support her through prayer and love. Ada did managed at church; she had always been one to stand straight and hold her head up through all kinds of shame, usually caused by Dewey, Sr. The Church Ladies soon found something else to gossip about, as they usually do in small towns.

It was partly Ada's fault Mary had joined the circus. Ada had once attended a circus as a young girl on a rare outing with her parents and often told the children bedtime stories about the animals and exciting exhibits. One story she told often was the one about the famous and largest elephant ever, Jumbo, who she had the privilege to see. She told how he had been bought by P.T. Barnum for his circus in America from the London Zoo and arrived by boat on the 25th of March, 1882, and for three years could be seen by American audiences. Sadly, she lamented, Jumbo was killed by a train as he was led to the circus wagons. His skeleton stands in the American Museum of National History as a monument to the circus world's most famous animal. This part she told with pride. She told the story so well the children often had tears in their eyes at the end. As a young girl, she had an old children's book with a circus theme. She read the book over and over again and often dreamed of herself as one of the glamorous Elephant Riders.

Once in the circus life, she found the money okay, not a lot, but more than she had ever made before. Nothing else was as promised; once on the road things changed. The nice trailer she was promised was in truth a very small one and she had to share it with three other girls, each having a narrow bunk and hardly any room to move around in. The outhouses were horrible, the showers usually cold, and the food was barely palatable to Mary's taste, as she was spoiled by Ada's good southern home cooking. When Mary first joined she was a healthy 130 pounds, and when she finally left she was a lean 115 pounds.

She enjoyed working with the elephants; they were just like big puppy dogs and she loved them. But the work was hard. They worked from sun up to sun down getting prepared for a show and closing down a show, and no one was idle. The people wore happy faces but most of them had tragic eyes. Some loved the work and knew they would never do anything else, but a lot of the younger girls had joined up in towns like Mary had, and were disappointed and hoped to escape soon. Mary knew some of them would not make it as the circus became a family for a lot of the people and they couldn't leave for the uncertainty of doing something different.

In the circus society there were positions of influence and power. One's station in the circus community depended on the act or job you performed. Of course there was the owner who sometimes traveled with the circus and other times stayed in the big cities to party a few more days with the people who invariably were attracted to the circus mystique. Many times the owner was away dealing with upcoming show locations. He was, most of the time, a horrible man. He was in his late fifties, not bad looking, with beautiful wavy white hair. He kept in pretty good shape; he was stocky with only a slight bulge around the middle. He had steel gray eyes, which could be mean or kind depending on whether he was mad at you or trying to seduce you into the circus life.

Then, there was the Ringmaster: tall, thin, almost stick thin, with jet black hair slicked back on his head from widow's peak, completing the look with a big black mustache in the handlebar fashion. In his red tuxedo jacket and top hat, he loved to sweep from his head across his body as he bowed, he cut quite a figure. He was a kind man but stern for he had to run the show when the owner was not there, or when the gentleman was indisposed because of partaking of too many spirits.

From there on, where you fit into the circus community depended on how big a draw or how dangerous, usually one in the same, your act was. The Flying Trapeze Artists were the kings and queens of the society, then the Lion Tamers, who often felt they were the kings, and competition for this title often led to desperate arguments and sometimes fisticuffs. These acts were arrogant and occupied the nicest trailers of the camp.

Then there was the High Wire Act and the performers who clowned or pirouetted on the tiny wire dangerously high above the crowds' cries of Whoa! Oh! The gasps filled the tent with appreciation, awe, and fear for the seemingly fearless actors.

Of course, the clowns, many wonderful older men who had made their life and home the circus, kept the crowd in stitches with their many talents and slapstick. Beautiful girls decked out in their decorative costumes rode the huge and much loved elephants and the prancing ponies. The elephants and clowns were the peg on which the circus was built, so many times the circus was judged on how many elephants the circus had. The more elephants the more famous the troupe would be. There were jugglers and tumblers and continuous music from the fantastic orchestra. The sound of vendors who wandered through the crowds barking "Peanuts, hotdogs, popcorn" all at one time added to the excitement and thrills that only the circus could bring.

The year Mary spent in the circus was to give her many experiences, some good and some bad, and consisted mostly of her traveling from city to town, nightly performances, hard work, making friends and enemies, and the pursuit and conquest of Demetrius. Some of these remembrances often, still, went through Mary's mind, and Dante caught her daydreaming again. He had picked her up after work and they were dining in the little café, when Mary's thoughts had wandered to that far away place.

"It's just about impossible to keep your attention."

"Oh, really, I am sorry, I do have a lot on my mind, but this was to be a dinner to take my mind off of things, and I apologize."

They returned to more interesting conversation. They were getting to know each other, were relaxed and each felt comfortable with the other, and felt they had know each other all their lives. It seemed they were destined to meet this time in their lives when both were alone and starting a new life in a new place and time.

Chapter 3

"Mary, I have had a wonderful time, I hope you have too!" He was watching her, waiting for a reaction; he smiled, and continued. "I would very much like to do this again."

"Dante, I have had the best time, and I would like to see you again. But for tonight it is getting late and . . ." she hesitated.

"I know, Cinderella, if I don't get you home before midnight you will turn into a pumpkin."

She laughed, "Yes, that is partly true, we are very busy at the store and I need the rest, although I hate to end this lovely evening, I must go."

"Can I pick you up after work for dinner tomorrow night?"

"I suppose so, if you are the gentleman you were tonight."

He had a twinkle in his eyes. "Do I detect a slight hesitation; I must assure you my interest in you is not for the short time pleasure." He smiled a smile that spoke volumes, and she doubted his words. She lowered her eyes and began fumbling with her purse.

'I hope you mean what you say Dante,' she thought 'because I would like to see more of you too.'

They spent the next few evenings together, again at the little café, once for hamburgers and once he took her to a Hollywood night club, the Earl Carroll Theatre Restaurant on Sunset Boulevard near Vine. A fantastic experience for Mary, as she had heard of the fame of Earl Carroll. He was an international celebrity. For years his name had been synonymous with the best on the American stage. His often paraphrased slogan, 'Through These Portals Pass the Most Beautiful Girls in the World,' had been honestly earned.

They had dressed for the occasion; Mary bought a new blue taffeta dress, the color of her eyes. Dante looked extremely handsome in a dark blue suit, light grey shirt and a red tie and handkerchief, folded nicely in his pocket, in honor of the Holiday Season.

It was the night before Christmas Eve, and a night to be forever remembered, with the lavish revue, it's all star cast, its unbelievable stage settings, its sensational double revolving stages, and its sixty most beautiful girls. Mary could not believe she was here with the glamorous Hollywood crowd. She wondered what the ladies at the Baptist Church would think about this, 'Who cares, they already have a low opinion of me anyway, although I do feel guilty, another glass of champagne will make me forget them, and all those other old biddies who walk around town like they never did anything wrong.'

Dante refilled her glass and she drank it fast. Her head was in a spin and she felt like she was on a roller coaster going a hundred miles an hour. Dante refilled her glass and offered a toast.

"Merry Christmas, and," he paused, "may all your Christmases be spent in the company of the glamorous and loved, with you being as admired and loved as you are right now."

She tried to offer a toast in return but her mind could not come up with one to match Dante's; she opened her mouth but nothing came out. She slowly brought the glass to her lips and sipped the champagne. 'I have to take this slowly; I am getting tipsy,' she thought.

Her eyes met his and she swallowed and hiccupped. He then suggested they spend Christmas Eve at his apartment, and he would cook dinner. Mary, now recovering from her embarrassment of the hiccup, her hand over her mouth, picked up her napkin and dabbed the moisture that had escaped her lips and finally answered him.

"I will not hear of it. I will buy the groceries and cook the dinner, if you want it to be at your place."

He said, "Okay but I bought a turkey and I will cook Christmas dinner for you."

She said, "You are too kind and you have spent too much money on me already." He said it was what he wanted to do, and spending time with her was worth it.

"Mary, if it wasn't for meeting you, I don't know what I would have done this Christmas."

Christmas Eve at the store was very busy. Mary picked out a nice tie and handkerchief for Dante and wrapped it prettily when she had a moment free. It would be a late evening and Mary still had to pick up groceries on the way home. She wanted to shower and get fixed up for the evening, so they had planned to meet at 9 p.m. at her house.

Beth had asked what she had planned for the evening as she had said she was too tired to do anything. Mary had answered that she should be tired, but she was too excited to be tired, that she was cooking for Dante at his apartment.

Beth gave her a sideways look and exclaimed, "At his apartment! My word! What does this mean?"

"Now Beth, I trust him, he's the first man I have trusted in a long time."

"Well, good luck. And have a great time. I think I am getting jealous, this guy sounds too good to be true."

Mary had the same thoughts. Her past experiences with men being disastrous. She was an affectionate and romantic woman who had not been able to express herself, being raised in a house where love between a man and a woman or a father and daughter was not expressed, and Ada always preaching the sins of sex before marriage.

Mary had avoided any romantic relationships. She had fed on romantic novels and wished for a romance, and then Luke had come along and asked her to marry him. He seemed to be interested in her for something other than the rest of the boys who were always trying to kiss her and touch her. She jumped at the chance; Luke was a very handsome young man. He had the blondest hair and greenest eyes; he was the class president, popular, and always had good manners.

This would be Mary's chance to get away from her oppressed home and start a romantic marriage.

A few months after they were married and had not fully consummated the union, she realized she had not loved him, but would have stayed out of duty and pity. He had often cried in her arms as a child would, asking for forgiveness, but not being able to tell her what was the matter with him.

Mary felt many times that it was her fault and tried to make it up to him with tenderness. After a year of this emotional turmoil, Luke asked her to divorce him, saying the problem was his and he had married her because of her beauty and kindness, and had hoped that he would have been better.

She was extremely hurt, but the request coming from him was a relief; she was too young and inexperienced to understand this complex problem. She had come to love him in her own way, like a brother she comforted.

She accepted his decision and went back home and filed for a divorce. And then there was Demetrius, what happened with him had left her completely disillusioned about men. Now Dante and her strong feelings for him, from the very beginning he had awakened those hidden feelings and had touched her as no man had before.

For dinner she had decided on something simple, because of the late hour and preparing it at his place: steaks, a nice salad, bread, baked potatoes, and a bottle of wine. It had taken all of the money she had left, as she had sent Ada some money with a Christmas card.

She would have to walk home from work instead of taking the bus, and take her lunch to work. She didn't mind.

She dressed fast but carefully. She wore a pretty white blouse with ruffles down the front, pearls around her neck and at her ears, a black straight skirt and black pumps. She was ready at five minutes to nine and was seated on the sofa with the shopping bag full of groceries on her lap waiting for Dante to arrive.

He arrived on time and when she answered the door with the bag of groceries in her arms, he took the bag from her, took a step back and surveyed her with his eyes. He placed the bag on the coffee table and took her into his arms and gave her a passionate kiss. She resisted slightly and then gave in to the passion. He left her weak in the knees.

He went over to the bag of groceries, picked it up and went directly to the refrigerator. "Change of plans," he said as he opened the refrigerator door and put the bag in. "I have plenty of food at home and I will not let you cook this late at night looking the way you do, don't protest, it is already settled."

Mary said, "I bought a good bottle of wine, can we take that?"

"Sure, I'll get it, you get your coat."

They drove to his apartment in silence; he lived in Glendale just over the hill from Hollywood, a duplex in a nice older neighborhood. The big old trees that lined the street reached each other overhead. Most of the houses were decorated with Christmas lights and some had Nativity scenes made out of plywood on their lawns. He said that tomorrow night he would take her for a drive around the city, and that there were streets where the decorations were famous to look at.

When they entered his apartment she was greeted with a beautifully decorated Christmas tree, and she realized why he had been so anxious for her to come there.

"My, you have been busy!" She was thrilled; she was grinning and began to laugh.

"I hope you are not laughing at me."

"No, no! I think it is wonderful. I just didn't expect it." She continued to giggle with delight. It had been a long time since she had been in a home with a Christmas tree and it brought back memories of happy times long ago.

"At my home we always had a Christmas celebration with all the family at my Mama and Papa's house and it seemed right to have a tree tonight." He touched her shoulders and turned her around to face him and gave her a tender kiss on her forehead, gazing into her eyes, "I'm glad you like it. Let's have a glass of that wine you brought to celebrate our first Christmas together."

"I have already prepared a light dinner of pasta and salad, which will only take a minute to put together, and I want you to open your presents first."

"Presents? You mean more than one?"

"Yes but only two."

"I hope you haven't overdone it."

He went into the kitchen to get the bottle of wine.

She was glad she had remembered to put the gift for him in her pocketbook, which she now removed and placed under the tree with the two packages that were already there.

He came back with the opened bottle of wine and two crystal glasses. He placed them on the table, took Mary by the hand and led her to the table, pulled out the chair for her and placed the two colorful packages on her lap. He then went to the phonograph and lifted the arm, as the voice of Bing Crosby filled the room with 'I'm Dreaming of a White Christmas.'

"I don't think we will have a white Christmas, but with you here it will not be as bleak as I thought it would be." He was sitting next to her and took her hands into his. "Mary I think I love you." She started to protest but he silenced her. "I know it seems too soon, but I haven't felt this way before. Mary, I wanted to take you in my arms the first time I laid my eyes on you." She could not reply, but she put her arms around him and held him with affection, she had tears in her eyes. He looked in to her eyes and said, "You don't have to say anything; I know it is too soon. Would you open your presents now?"

"Okay," she dabbed at her eyes with the back of her hand.

"Open the big box first." he said with a big smile.

She proceeded to take the paper off of the box and then unfold the tissue paper. There was the red velvet dress she had admired in the window of the department store on the day they had met.

She gasped "You didn't? How could you know I loved this dress? This is too much!"

"No it isn't, take it out and hold it up, I want to see how it will look on you." She did and he just smiled.

She went to him and hugged him. "You are just too nice to me. I love it, of course. You knew I would, didn't you?"

"I hoped, open the little box."

She did and there in the little box were little rhinestone earrings that matched the buttons on the front of the dress. "Oh! These are just perfect."

"I want you to wear the dress and earrings tomorrow; we are going to have a special Christmas.

"Oh Dante, I think I love you too." He kissed her softly and she responded. Then, he lifted her and carried her in to the bedroom, the Christmas presents, the wine, and the dinner forgotten.

Afterwards, she turned away from him and started crying softly, a heartbreaking kind of sorrowful sound. Dante put his arm around her and said, "What's wrong? I do love you, you know."

"I love you too."

"Then how can anything be wrong."

"Oh Dante, it's, it's, just that I am so ashamed."

"Please don't be, I love you and I want to marry you."

"Marry me?"

"Yes, that is what I was going to ask you tonight, Mary, will you marry me?"

Mary was sitting up in bed with the cover pulled up to her neck with an astonished look on her face. The tears stopped abruptly.

She got a sheepish grin on her face. "You want to marry me?"

"I do."

"But it's too soon."

"Do you love me?"

"Oh yes."

"Then it's not too soon. Think about it while I fix us that dinner I promised you. He got off the bed and took a couple of robes out of the closet and tossed one at her, she caught it and laughed at him.

"Okay mister, you are really funny."

She put on the robe. It was way too big for her, but she held it up, and with her pocketbook in hand went into the bathroom to freshen up. She looked at herself in the mirror and saw a girl flushed with happiness. Then reality came back to her. The look on her face saddened as she tried to put lipstick on, 'I can't do this to him, he doesn't know me, he has put me on a pedestal, and to him, and I am not what I am. Oh dear God forgive me, I am so sorry. What have I done?' Sadly she finished and went to find Dante.

She found him in the kitchen singing Italian Opera as he held a piece of spaghetti up on a fork to test for tenderness. He turned, bowed to her and said, "Come into my kitchen, we are almost ready, you can help me toss the salad."

"Dante, we have to talk. I didn't mean for it to happen that way, I just got caught up in the moment."

"Well isn't that the way it is supposed to happen?" he said as he gazed at her.

"Please, there are things you do not know about me."

"I know all that I need to know about you. I love you."

"It's important that I tell you about myself."

"You already told me. Didn't you?"

"Yes some, but not all. I didn't think things would go this far, and where things stand right now, you have to know the rest."

"Okay, but can't it wait until after we eat dinner?"

"Okay, but then you have to listen to me."

"I will. Don't look so sad. I am sure it's nothing that can change the way I feel about you."

She went into the dining room and poured the two glasses of wine, noticing the intricate design of the crystal glasses.

"Were these glasses your mothers?" she guessed.

"Yes, they were. She let me have them to take away with me so I wouldn't forget home, as if I could."

"You will have to tell me all about them."

"I will. They will love you."

'Oh, I hope you will love me still; forget about the family, after I tell you about myself.' She thought as she sat forlornly down in the dining room chair to wait for Dante.

He entered carrying two plates of salad and they ate in silence, Mary barely getting the chunks of lettuce down. He then went into the kitchen to get the pasta,

"Can I help you?" Mary asked.

"No, just let me wait on you. You can help me tomorrow with the Christmas turkey." He had noticed her unease and sadness, but he didn't understand it.

He sat the plates on the table overflowing with spaghetti and red sauce.

"This is really good." The sauce was surprisingly good, rich in spices, tangy, and satisfying.

Mary realized she was ravishingly hungry. She sucked a strand of spaghetti into her mouth, the end flicking her on the forehead and leaving a trail of sauce across her face. She smiled as she lifted her napkin to clean her face.

"Is there a special way to eat this stuff so that I don't make a fool of myself?"

'Why am I always so clumsy around you,' she thought.

"Here let me show you." He laughed. "Yes, there is. You must take that big spoon by your plate, take a little of the pasta on your fork in your right hand and with the spoon in your left hand roll the spaghetti around in it and there you have a perfect mouthful," he said, as he demonstrated to her.

She tried it and then she smiled at him.

"You still have a little sauce on your nose," he said.

Embarrassed, she again wiped her nose with the napkin.

"You missed, here let me get it." And he did, tenderly.

After dinner, he led her back into the bedroom. She protested this time, saying that they had to talk, that she had to go home. He said not now, that she belonged there tonight; it was too cold to go out and oh so warm in the bed. It was very late and Mary was suddenly very tired, the thought of getting into the discussion about her past was far from her mind. They cuddled under the warm blankets and slept in peace.

The next morning, she awoke feeling very cozy in the large bed. She was alone and the thoughts of the night before came rushing back. 'Oh my God, oh God, what am I going to do, I am so ashamed. Please God, help Me.' she prayed. She cried. And she seemed to hear from God 'If you tell the truth all will be well.' 'Okay' she thought. She got out of bed and went to take a shower. She could hear Dante in the kitchen banging around pots and pans and humming that same tune he was singing the night before. She recognized it as 'O Solo Mio.' Hearing his cheerful humming she thought, 'It's Christmas morning. What could go wrong? I'll just tell him the truth, I love him too. I know it now, and if he still loves me, I will marry him.' Then she realized the truth would ruin everything.

After breakfast he started to clean the dishes, but she took his hand and led him into the living room, and directed him to sit on the sofa. She sat down beside him and asked him to please listen to her. He said he knew all he needed to know. That he knew she was beautiful and sweet and that was all that mattered.

"I do realize you were not a virgin. I must admit I thought you would be. You are so young and a country girl, but I am not disappointed. I'm not a complete idiot; I've been around a little myself. I love you and my parents will love you, too. Mary, I want to marry you and I want to do it as soon as possible."

"I love you, too. How could I not," she said as tears came flooding into her eyes.

"But I cannot marry you. You are Catholic, aren't you?"

"Yes, but what does that have to do with getting married?" He asked with disappointment in his voice.

"I have been married before." She blurted out. This brought him to his feet.

"Married before, how? How can that be?" He was dumbfounded.

"I was divorced a little over a year ago. I lived with Luke for a year. I married him to get out of the house. My family life was not good," she paused. Tears were coming fast now. She continued with difficulty.

"Luke was kind to me and he was different from the other boys I knew. So, when he asked me to marry him I accepted. On our wedding night nothing happened, and for the year we were married we never made love. Not even once. I knew this was not right, if I was going to be married I wanted children, so I left him and went back home. My parents never knew why I left him, but they didn't approve of the marriage anyway and wanted me back home. They thought I was too young to get married. My Mama only gave her consent because she knew how unhappy I was at home."

"But?" he questioned.

"Oh there's more. It's hard for me to tell you the rest but you have to know. I joined the Circus six months later, things at home were not any better and I saw the Circus as a way out of Texas and a way to get away from my Daddy."

"Your Father?"

"Oh it's not what you are thinking, he was abusive but not in that way. I left my mother a note and left before anyone was awake. There was a man there who wanted me and pursued me, he wouldn't leave me alone. It only happened once. I didn't love him; I only think I was lonely and starved for affection." She looked at him, he had sat at the table and his head was bent and held in his hands.

"I'll leave," she said.

She went in to the bedroom to get her clothes which were scattered around the room. She sat on the bed in very much the same position she had left Dante, with her head in her hands and wept softly.

He came into the room, sat down beside her, put his arm around her shoulder and took her into his arms. He said softly, "Don't cry, Mary. We all make mistakes, I don't judge you. If you will marry me the only problem I can see is that we will not be able to get married in the Catholic Church."

"What about your parents?" She looked into his eyes and saw only love.

"Oh, they will raise a fuss I'm sure, about not getting married in the Church. They are old country, but they will come around, they are good people; they will love you as I do."

"I do want to marry you, Dante, I have never felt like this before, I don't want to lose you." she said passionately.

He kissed away her salty tears. "It's settled then; we'll get married on New Year's Eve and start our new life on the New Year."

Chapter 4

The next morning they showered and went into the kitchen to prepare the Christmas turkey. They prepared the stuffing. He stuffed the turkey and put it in the oven to bake. She said she had to go home for awhile. He asked her why and she told him she had to get a few things. He told her everything she needed was already there; he wanted her to wear the red dress today. They both dressed nicely. He said she looked like a Christmas angel in the pretty red dress. Her hair, washed many times and fluffed lightly around her face, added to the image.

They sat at the dining room table with cups of tea, to plan and talk and wait for the turkey to be done. She remembered the gift she had for him, and went and got it from under the tree and gave it to him. He opened it and said he hadn't expected anything. He told her it was beautiful and he loved it. He kissed her. She said she wanted to know about his family, and she wanted to call her mother before the day was over. He said he wanted to tell her about his family and that he had to call home also.

"Okay," he stated, taking a sip of his tea before continuing, "My parents are from Italy, a town called Benevento, near Naples. My father and his brother came to the United States first from Italy to make enough money to send for their wives and children. They parted almost immediately; my father's brother had connections here from the old country who gave them jobs. My Papa started work in the garment district. He had talent as an artist, and soon became a designer of women's coats. The family business in Italy was making shoes. He sent for my Mama and my three brothers and my sister. My mother had eight children, two died at birth, and one of my brothers died on the way from Italy on the boat. He wasn't strong enough to make the trip. I was born here in America, somewhere between New York and New Jersey. My parents were traveling when my mother came into labor and they stopped at a country doctor's home where I was born. Mama had another little baby boy after me and now I have three brothers and a sister.

I am the only one to leave New York. My Papa did well with the coat business, by then he had his own line of women's coats. I think they are wonderful people and I miss them a lot, especially today. My brothers and I were every close. We were always getting into mischief and driving my Mama crazy. My sister Josephine was a blessing to my mother, with us four boys driving her crazy, Joe was always there to help her. I can imagine them; everyone gathered at Papa's house, drinking wine and eating all day. I wish we were there now so they could meet you," he smiled affectionately at her. "How's that for a quick story."

"It's a good story, except for the babies dying that makes me sad," she answered. "They sound like a close family." Dante's love for his family was evident in the telling of the story. "Yes, my Mama went through a lot, but back then, babies surviving, was not as easy as it is today."

"We are a close family so it was hard for me to leave them, but I wanted to see the country. I drove from New York across the country with a couple of my friends, who like me, were a little crazy. I ended up here, and it was probably the weather and the job opportunities that made me stay." He took her hand in his. "Now I have found you and I think we will make California our home. Now, tell me about your family."

"Well, my story, I'm sorry to say, is not about a happy family. My Daddy, who I do love, drinks too much. When he is sober, he is a good man, but those times are few and far between. We lived very poorly. My father had a hard time keeping a job. My mother had to take in laundry and work hard to help out. The sad news is that they broke up. In fact, the letter that made me so sad this week was from my mother, Ada, she told me she is staying at her brother's house now, and that my younger brother, who isn't even 18 years old yet, joined the Navy." Tears were welling up in her eyes and she desperately wanted to end the family story.

But she pressed on. "You know the Circus story and how I ended up here; I came here because Hollywood sounded exciting."

"Let's call home," he said. Dante could see that Mary needed to talk to her mother right then. "You call your mother first, and tell her about us. I want her to come out here for our wedding. I'll send her a train ticket. You're going to live here now and she can live in your apartment. I am doing well financially and we can help her out." He said this with great enthusiasm.

"You mean it; she can come to California to live? Oh! That would be wonderful. I know she is lonely now. I have been worried about her and I would love to have her close."

"I think it is the only answer, we need her too. I want us to have a good family, she sounds like a wonderful mother and she will be around when we have babies."

"Babies, you mean babies right away?"

"Yes Babies."

"I hope not too soon."

"We'll see."

She wrapped her arms around him; a lump in her throat. "Thank you, Dante, thank you."

She went to the phone and dialed the long distant phone number. Uncle Henry answered. "Uncle Henry? It's Mary, Merry Christmas. How is everyone?"

"We are all fine now, we sure miss you though. How are y'all out there?"

"I'm fine here too. Can I speak to Mama? I have some good news for her."

"Well she could sure use some good news right now. I'll get her and Merry Christmas to you too."

She heard him calling her mother's name and Ada answering. "My Mary's on the phone! Oh, God bless her. Mary, Mary, is that you? I hoped you would call but didn't expect it. Where are you calling from? Did you get a Phone?"

"Mama it's me, Merry Christmas." She could hear Ada crying now. "Mama, please don't cry. I know things have been bad but they are about to get better. I've got some good news, can you hear me?"

"I can hear you. I miss you so much, when are you coming home?"

"Mama, I'm not coming home, you are coming out here to California to live with me." She paused, but there was no reaction from Ada. "I'm getting married to a wonderful man and he wants you to come out here and live close to us." She paused again and waited.

"I'm coming out there? You're getting married? I don't understand, what you mean by all this?"

"Just what I said; I met a man, a wonderful man, and we are getting married on New Year's Eve. And he wants you to come out here to be with us. He is going to send you a train ticket, and you have to bring everything with you. You are going to stay here."

"Mary, it's too much, I can't think!"

"It's all settled, you don't have to think about it. You can't stay with Uncle Henry forever and we have a place for you here. We are going to start a family. I'll call you tomorrow with all the details." She smiled at Dante. "Mama, don't worry it will be alright, I promise."

Ada was crying again. "Oh, Mary I am so happy for you, and me coming out there I can't believe it."

"Its true, Mama, please don't worry. Have a good Christmas day and I will call you tomorrow."

"Okay, Mary, I just can't believe this right now."

"You will, Mama," she paused, "I love you, good bye for now."

"How did she take it?" Dante asked.

"Oh, she is confused, but she will do it. She needs help making decisions right now. With the decisions she has made about my Daddy and CL, she is questioning everything she has done. And I think this is the right thing for her now. I am so happy you are bringing her here. I have been so worried about her. She tries to hide how she is feeling, but she is very lonely and upset." She paused. "I have to warn you, she can be difficult sometimes. She is a strict Southern Lady and very opinionated at times, but she is the kindest person in the world, with a heart of pure gold."

"She's your mother and I know it will be all right."

He took the phone from her and called his family. He looked at Mary and smiled a sheepish grin. "My turn."

His mother answered the phone. "Ma, it's Dante.

"*Mio Figliuolo, Dante?*"

"*Si*, Merry Christmas! I'm getting married." He blurted out laughing.

"*CIO Che!*"

"*Matrimonio, Ma!*"

"*Matrimonio? Ella Buono!*"

"*Si, Ma Moltto buono, alto che? Non ho visto uno donna cosi bella dall'ultima volt ache ho guardato le illustranzioni un libro de fate.*"

"*E' buonissimo, Dante?*"

"*Oh si', e' buonissimo.*"

"*Sono contento, addio, mia amore'*, Merry Christmas." She hung up.

"What happened?" Mary asked.

"It was my Ma and she is emotional. My Papa will call back."

"What did you tell her about me?"

"I told her you were a nice girl and that you were as pretty as an angel in a fairytale."

The phone rang and it was his father. He had to get all the details. He wanted to know if they were

59

getting married in the Catholic Church; if Mary was Catholic.

And Dante told him, "No, she is not Catholic and we are just going to have a small civil service." His father was disappointed and didn't say anything for a while. "Papa, she is perfect, beautiful and kind, you will love her."

His father said, "If you are happy, we will be happy for you." Dante talked to his sister, then his brother, and told them as soon as they were settled they would come home for a trip to see everybody. When he hung up, Dante and Mary were both smiling.

Chapter 5

They were married on New Year's Eve. Ada didn't make it for the wedding, but arrived one week later. She had started her divorce before she left Texas and was quickly settled into Mary's apartment.

Dante and Mary met Ada at the train station in Glendale. They saw each other at the same time. She hurried carrying her suitcase and packages to meet them.

"Mary! Oh! Let me look at you! You have changed your hair. Well my, my, my, it's so different, but you always look pretty!"

"Oh, Mama, you look so wonderful." The two women hugged each other as packages dropped unnoticed to the ground.

They were both chocked up with tears. Dante just stood there taking it all in; he had picked up the forgotten packages and was holding them for Ada. He thought 'Now there is a woman from the deep south!' Ada just grinned at him through her tears. Her speech was as slow, thick and sweet, as a humid summer night laced with the smell of Magnolia blossoms.

Mary took Ada's hand and led her to face Dante. "Mama, this is my husband Dante."

Ada caught her breath as she looked up into his soft brown eyes. She was speechless, a very rare exception for Ada. He lifted her chin and placed a kiss on each wet cheek, and then he smiled his glorious smile. He then gave her a gentle hug. Ada staggered a little; she was very tired from the long train ride and taken aback with the charm of Dante.

"My goodness sake! You are tall! I am very glad to meet ya. Thank you so much for sending me the train ticket." She poked Mary and whispered to her, "I had no Idea! He is so handsome, Mary, but he does have those brown eyes."

"Mama, will you never change." She laughed.

Mary and Dante had worked all morning to prepare a nice dinner at their place and had left up all the Christmas decorations, including the tree, in honor of Ada's arrival and the missing of celebrating Christmas together.

Mary could tell Ada was totally bedazzled by Dante's charms. He had complimented her by saying he knew where Mary got her good looks, and how she was going to have a hard time fighting off all of the admirers she was sure to attract. There were a hungry lot of men in this part of the country he joked. She blushed and giggled, and thoroughly enjoyed herself and the belated Christmas with Mary and Dante.

Ada got a job at Gladding Mc Bean working in the factory packing dishes in boxes for shipping. It was a twenty minute ride on the bus from the apartment and it worked out well. Most times when Dante or Mary was able, they picked her up and brought her back to Dante's duplex to have dinner with them.

She seemed happy enough. She worried about CL but she and Mary tried to keep in touch with him through the mail. He was on a ship in the South Pacific. He had written that he had never worked so hard, but he was adjusting. He said he enjoyed being out on the ocean-the gentle rolling of the waves, the salt air. He had never even seen the ocean before joining the Navy.

He also told of storms and everyone getting sick, and rolling around on deck or below deck, holding onto their bunks in the worst of the storms. He didn't talk of the battles, or the men who suffered death or maiming.

The first couple of months of Mary and Dante's marriage were great; they went out a lot. Dante enjoyed taking Mary dining and dancing at the nightclubs around town. He had taken her shopping and bought her pretty dresses for just such occasions. He wanted to show her off. It gave him pleasure. They made a striking couple and danced many nights away.

They had dinner at the Brown Derby on Wilshire Boulevard-reservations made well in advance. Mary couldn't believe the restaurant was actually built like a derby at the entrance, and marveled at the portraits of the stars on the walls. She actually recognized Gene Kelly sitting at a table under which his portrait was hanging. He was enjoying his dinner with a beautiful starlet by his side.

They spent evenings alone, and evenings with Ada, and Ada insisted they have Sunday dinner after church at her new apartment. They were establishing their own little family. For Dante only one thing was missing.

"Yes. I think I am," said Mary.

"How long has it been? Why haven't you told me?" Dante asked.

"I was worried. It's too soon, and I was afraid how you would react."

They had been sitting on the side of the bed and Dante folded her in his arms.

"Don't be silly," he said. "I love you. I want a family more than anything. I'm very happy." He then took her face and placed kisses all over her cheeks and lips.

"I'll be fat and ugly," she moaned.

"You will never be ugly to me, how can the mother of my children ever be ugly. Are you sure you are pregnant?"

"Yes, Dante, I went to the doctor yesterday."

"Are you as happy as I am?"

"Oh, yes, Dante. If it makes you this happy then I will be happy."

But Mary didn't want to start a family this soon; she had been enjoying the night life and knew this would have to end now that she was pregnant.

Mary accepted her pregnancy with Dante's encouragement, and they settled into a more quiet life. He was constantly watching her so she would not overdo it.

Chapter 6

Ada, being an attractive woman in her own right, had met a man at work, and he was courting her. They spent quiet dinners out with Dante and Mary and he joined them at the Sunday dinners.

Ada had been through a lot and the companionship of a man who gave her attention and showered her with small gifts and flowers was very exciting to her.

She had had many sleepless night worrying and suffering guilt over her divorce of Dewey Sr. No one in her family had ever gotten a divorce before and the shame and embarrassment and religious implications haunted her continuously. She was sure she was going to hell. But she prayed every night for God to forgive her and please watch over CL, and let Mary's baby be alright. She now felt it had been a rash decision, she lamented. She should have waited, she cried. Then her intelligence told her that there had never been any other way if she and CL were to survive.

She had learned to live with Dewey Sr. drinking and his frequent affairs with other women, but his abuse of CL and the times he had threatened them with a gun were more than anyone could be expected to live with. She remembered the times he had come home drunk out of his mind. He would get them all out of bed and make them sit on the sofa together while he sat in a chair in front of them with a gun pointed at them and he would say, "If anyone of you moves I will shoot you into the next county." He would scowl at them and say, "You are all mine and don't anyone of you ever think of leaving me." Then the next morning he would act like nothing had happened the night before. Ada and the children walked around in shock for a few days, but Dewey Sr. didn't even notice.

She had been told by others that she was too good of a woman to take the treatment she had been taking and that she had to think of her children. They had seen bruises on her arms and one time, a black eye. But when she applied for a divorce many of the friends who had told her this, looked at her with disapproval, because many people did like the charming Dewey, and didn't know how deep the hurt went.

At first the attentions of a new man worried her, as she didn't think she was worthy of love. Dewey Sr. had made sure she had lost all self confidence. But soon she accepted them as a possible answer to her prayers.

Ada had sharper features than Mary, she had an aristocratic nose and pretty blue eyes, and she always wore nice dresses, never leaving home without her corset. She carried herself, as she would if nothing was ever wrong, with her head held high and perfect posture as she was taught my her mother.

Dante had taken her shopping one Saturday afternoon, she protested, but graciously accepted when he insisted she should have the latest fashions. She insisted she would keep the receipts and pay him back as soon as possible. It had been a long time since anyone had fussed over her and she was thrilled.

Earl Dagon, a slightly rotund, prematurely bald man, was her supervisor at Gladding Mc Bean. He had never been married and at this time in his life he was looking for a wife.

When he met Ada he knew right away she would make a good wife. He liked her laugh, her neatness and her cooking most of all.

He owned a nice large home in Glendale and this attracted Ada, as she had not had a home of her own since the fire. The places she lived in since then had, although she always made them nice, had been run down and cheap and not her own.

He asked her to marry him and six months later they were married in a civil service at the city hall with Mary and Dante as witnesses. Then they had a small celebration at Earl's home afterwards. Ada had worn a nice blue suit, a white blouse and a pretty hat with flowers on it, and Earl looked very distinguished in a pinstriped suit and light blue shirt. They seemed very happy.

Mary never did get big or fat, she gained very little weight, and most people didn't even know she was pregnant. She never wore maternity clothes and worked up until two weeks before her due date which was November 1st. On the 30th of October, being precarious as she was, she decided she wanted her baby to be born on Halloween.

Halloween being a quasi holiday of course, was the one in which she had had the most fun through her life. Without Dante knowing, she bundled herself up in her camel coat and went to the drug store on the corner and ordered a 'Castor Oil Cocktail,' which in those days was believed to bring on labor. It did and at 6 a.m. the next morning, without much trouble, she delivered a six pound, one ounce, baby girl.

She was resting, half awake when Dante entered the room, grinning from ear to ear. She smiled at him and said weakly, "Did you see her? I know you wanted a boy, but she is beautiful isn't she? I heard the doctor say she was the prettiest baby he has seen in a long time."

"Yes, I saw her and she is beautiful. I think she smiled at me. I'm not disappointed at all. I have loved her since the day I knew you were going to have a baby. I can't believe all that hair!"

"I'm pretty sure that is from your side of the family. My Mama said we were born with heads as bald as raw eggs." But the nurses said it would all fall out. Did you see the pink ribbon they had already put in her hair?"

They named the baby Maryanna, after the grandma's, Dante's mothers' name was Antoinette Maria, and Ada's middle name was Mary. They would call her Anna. She was born with three-inch dark brown curls-which she did lose, she had long black lashes with big dark eyes. She was plump for being such a small baby; she had a healthy pink complexion and rosy cupid bow lips.

Ada arrived with Earl, laden with gifts for the baby and a pink fluffy bed jacket for Mary. Ada proceeded to fawn over and admire their first grandchild.

Their first Christmas together was spent at Earl and Ada's house. Ada had gone all out to make it a festive and joyous occasion. The six-week old baby was doted on by all. Pictures were taken to send to New York of the happy couple and the little baby girl, the first baby girl grandchild for Dante's parents.

His sister, Josephine, and her husband, Larry, had two boys, and his brother, Vincent II, and his wife, Esther, had a boy, named Vincent James III, called, Vinnie Jr., Josephine's boys, Johnny being two years old and their Vincent, called Vinnie, being one years old. Dante's younger brother, Antonio, was married to

Gloria, and they had a boy named, Richard, called Richie, and he was also one years old. All the one year old boys were born within months of each other.

Anna had received many gifts from the family back east; pretty dresses it would take months for Anna to grow into, and dolls bigger than she was. It was evident this baby would be spoiled by all the family.

Dante called her his princess. He said, "Well I am the King, don't I sit on my throne every morning?" He would always laugh when he said this, referring to the time he spent in the bathroom with the newspaper each morning. Anna would smile and a twinkle would always be in her eyes for everybody.

The only sad part of this Christmas day was, no news from CL, not for a long time: Mary noticed Ada with an occasional faraway look in her eyes and they would exchange sad thoughts. Prayers were said for him at dinner and they all consumed the best turkey they had ever eaten.

The very next Saturday, Ada phoned Mary and asked her to come over to the house. She had received a letter from CL, and she wanted Mary to be able to read it herself. Mary asked her if it was bad news, shaking already, and Ada answered her saying it was okay news and not to worry.

Relieved, Mary bundled Anna up in a pretty pink sweater and matching bonnet with many blankets against the chill. It was a cloudy day and threatening rain, but she wanted to walk. It was only a few blocks from Dante's duplex to Earl's house. Dante was busy with some work he had brought home from the office. He told her to go ahead and call her when she was ready to come home and he would come and get her.

She arrived at the house a little chilled, the sky had threatened to open up with a few claps of thunder and a swift wind pushed her the last block. Ada met her at the open door and Mary followed her into the cozy kitchen where cups of hot tea were waiting. There on the table was CL's letter. Ada took baby Anna from Mary's arms and smiled at her, coo-chi-cooing her as the baby responded with a smile and a coo for her Grandma.

They sat down at the table and Mary read CL'S letter:

Dear Mama and Mary,

I received your letters and I am happy for the both of you and I can hardly wait to get home to meet the new men in your lives and meet my new niece. I'm sorry I haven't written sooner, I have been on a tour of the islands and we saw a lot of action. I saw some of my friends get hurt and we did have a rough time of it for a while. But don't worry I am alright. I can't tell you much about it right now because of security, our letters are monitored. Someday I might be able to talk about it, I don't know, I didn't know it would be like this. I have seen so much, I guess I have grown up a lot in the past year.

Anyway, I am in Hawaii now, can you believe it? I am at Pearl Harbor, thank God I wasn't here a couple of years ago; the people here will never get over what happened here. But it is

the most beautiful place I have ever seen. I
have been exploring every chance I get and it is
truly paradise.

I have met a girl, her name is Mildred, her
father is an Admiral stationed here and she is
known as a 'Navy Brat.' She had lived in many
places. I might be in love; she has long brown
hair and is very pretty. Don't be surprised if I
announce wedding plans of my own soon.

I am scheduled to go out again soon. I can't
tell you where or when, but I will write again as
soon as I can.

Again, congratulations to both of you. It sounds
like our family is doing better finally, my love to
all of you. I miss you all so much, but having
Mildred makes things better.

Love, CL

PS: The picture included is me and Mildred at
Pearl Harbor.

"He's got a girl! Let me see the picture." She
extended her hand to Ada. Ada reached into her pocket
where she had put the picture; she took it out
reluctantly, as if she couldn't part with it. She reached
into the other pocket for a tissue as the tears were
coming.

"He looks so handsome in his uniform!" She
gushed as she dabbed her eyes.

Mary gazed at the picture-at the handsome couple-CL did indeed look handsome in his Navy whites and the girl next to him did look pretty in a plump sort of way. The smiles were genuine. CL looked to have grown taller and he was so handsome with his wavy blonde hair and blue eyes just like Mary's. He had a fine physique, and in spite of the troubles he had he was always wearing a big grin with the deepest dimples in each cheek.

Mary often felt that her father couldn't understand that CL just couldn't help smiling so much, and if infuriated him. She would chide CL and tell him not to smile so much around Daddy, but he couldn't help it, it was his nature, and it hurt Mary to think that some day her daddy could break his wonderful spirit.

"They do look nice together; do you think he will marry her?" Mary asked.

"Well, I guess only time will tell. It's good to hear from him, but I still can't stop worrying about him all the time."

"I know Mama, me too. There is so much we do not know about the war and he can't tell us. We just have to pray and pray and hope God let's him come home to us."

There was a pause in the conversation and Mary took a look around the house. Earl had given Ada carte blanche to fix the house up the way she wanted, and Ada had worked her magic on the place. The house had really needed a woman's touch and the whole house now was warm and lovely.

The house sat on one lot and the other lot next was also owned by Earl, which was a complete garden. There was a huge flowering tree; bare now for the winter, and the rest of the garden was overgrown.

Ada had noticed Mary looking around and she said, "Do you like what I have done to the house? I have to start on the garden next. I'll have the prettiest flower garden in the neighborhood." Mary laughed and thought, 'I hope that's not the only reason you married Earl.'

"Mama, I know you will have the best garden and I love the house, you have done wonders with it; it was so dark before and you opened it up and it is cheerful and warm. I think it is great, and I am very happy for you, you deserve the best." She hugged her mother. "I love you so much, Mama, and I want you to be so happy."

"What do you hear from back home?" Mary asked. She had been wondering about her Daddy, she knew Ada wrote to her sister and brothers and that they knew about what was going on with Dewey Sr.

"Your Daddy has been writing me," Ada answered, understanding Mary's inquiry.

"What!" She said in disbelief, "I thought that was all over."

"With your Daddy it will never be over until one of us is dead. He says he is very sorry and wants me back. Your Uncle Henry says he has stopped drinking and has a good job, but you know this has happened before whenever I threatened to leave him. Things would be good for a time, but he always went back to his old ways when he knew he had me back again. I must admit, he does sound sincere this time, I don't know what he expects me to do; he knows I am remarried, but he doesn't seem to care. I wish he would just leave me alone. It makes me wonder if I made the right decision."

"Mama, you know you did the right thing, don't let him ruin what you have now with these doubts. You know how charming and persuasive he can be when he wants to be. Don't ever question what you did; what you did was for your survival."

"He wants to see the baby and he wants to see you. He says he is the babies Granddaddy. He says he is sober now and has the right to see his Grandbaby."

"I don't know if he deserves anything from any of us, Mama. You know I still love him, he's my Daddy, and there were some good years. He did try, and I know sometimes things were just too hard for him, but I just don't know. There are some things I can never forgive."

"Think about it, Mary, we could take a trip back to Mississippi. I miss my family and my mother is not well. I don't know that she will survive very much longer and I would like to see her before it's too late. We can go to Texas and stay at Uncle Henrys a few days, I miss him too. Then, we can go to Mississippi for a few days to see the rest of the relatives. What do you think? I am pretty sure Earl would let me go; he knows how much I miss the family."

'This could be the reason behind it all' Mary thought. Ada was the oldest of 10 children and her parents were still alive, but not well, in Mississippi. After they were married, Ada and Dewey Sr. had gone with

Uncle Henry to Texas to find work. Henry and Dewey Sr. had been boyhood friends. Mary promised to talk it over with Dante.

"Oh, I found something of yours when I moved here from your apartment, you must have overlooked it; it was on the shelf in the closet in the very back." Ada got up to find the lost object. Mary picked up the baby who had been sleeping in the baby buggy and held her in her lap until Ada came back. She was trying to remember what it could be that she left in the apartment. She remembered the Circus stuff! The box of collected momentums from the places she had visited and pictures of her friends from the year she had spent in the Circus. 'Oh my God,' she thought 'just what I need now, I hope she hasn't looked in the box.' This was a sore spot between the two women and best forgotten.

Ada returned with the box in hand. "It's a pretty wooden box with beautiful inlay on top." She looked at Mary and Mary blushed and reached for the box.

"Thank you, Mama. I had forgotten all about that box." This was the only explanation she offered and then she rose and headed for the phone. "I told Dante I would call him to pick me up."

The storm had hit with full force as the day had passed. The women had barely noticed; engrossed as they were in their conversation, but now both embarrassed about who may have looked in the box and the other who may be hiding something from her mother. They remarked now on the weather and how it could rain so hard in sunny California.

They seated themselves on the newly upholstered sofa, matching legs crossed. Mary was bouncing the baby on her knee and Ada was tickling her under the chin, both using the baby as a distraction while they waited for Dante to arrive.

PART TWO

THE CIRCUS

Chapter 7

That night Mary could not sleep remembering her time in the Circus she had put most of the memories away with the box of momentums now that the box was back, so were the memories. She got up out of bed, peeked at the sleeping baby who had been sleeping restful all night, and went into the living room closet where the box was now stored on the shelf. She had put the box there when she put away the coats. Dante had not seen her do this so she had not had to explain it to him. She tiptoed to the sofa and turned on the lamp; she listened quietly for a moment and could hear Dante snoring lightly and knew he would not wake up.

She opened the box and started to remove the contents one at a time. The first was a picture of her on her elephant, Bingo – a good picture. No one knows how it feels to be riding so high up on the massive animal, as it sways back and forth while dressed like the Queen of Sheba, and the applause of the crowd roaring in their ears, unless they have done it. It was very exciting, and she remembered her fond feelings for the elephant. She had matchbooks from places she had been and napkins from restaurants from all over the country. There were so many pictures, pictures of other performers who were her friends, pictures of the Flying Trapeze artists; Demetrius, arrogant smiling face, sent chills down her spine; remembering both the good and the bad.

The day Mary had visited the circus with her friend, Gail, had been a very exciting day for her. It had been an especially hot and humid summer; a thunderstorm in the afternoon had cooled the temperatures a bit but added to the humidity that day. Trying to keep the perspiration from their brows, the two girls dressed carefully with anticipation for the evening ahead. Both girls wore fluffy summer frocks and crimped their hair with the curling irons. It was to be the Circus' last performance in their little town in Texas, and they had saved their tips earned at their waitress jobs at the diner; where they both worked, to pay for the admission.

They had watched the promotional parade from the window of the diner as it came noisily down Main Street. There were elephants, seemingly an endless amount of the stupendous animals with their fine ivory tusks. The shouts of the crowd along the sidewalk cheered, "Here come the elephants-count them!" All of this had fueled their excitement. The two young girls could hardly wait until the afternoon they were to have off to go.

At first view of the big top and decorative front festooned with hundreds of tiny lights, the two girls grabbed each other's hands and smiled at one another, shimmers of excitement were completely evident as they handed their tickets to the taker and entered the big top. Immediately upon entering the tent and seeing part of the performance Mary began to devise a plan. Halfway through the show, she excused herself from Gail telling her she had to go to the ladies room, which was true, but she also wanted to visit the owner and ask him about joining the circus.

Out of the tent and walking down the midway of concessions of food, games of chance and the fortune-teller's booth, she saw a funny little man. She suspected he was a dwarf, he was dressed as a droll; she noticed through his makeup that he had an exceptionally big nose and that his eyes bulged out. He was staring at her as she was staring at him.

"Can I help you?" The little man asked.

"Yes, please. I was looking for the owner of the circus." The funny little man bowed from the waist and removed his pointed hat with a sweeping gesture.

"Peg at your service." Here, let me take your hand and escort you to the master's palace. His name is John McNamara, but mostly everyone calls him Mac; you'd better call him Mr. McNamara if you are looking for a job. That is what you are doing, isn't it?"

"Well, you guessed right. Thank you, it would be my pleasures to have you escort me, Mr. Peg."

He took her hand with a big grin and she followed him down the midway. They reached the festively painted wagon trailer, he led her up the stairs, stood on tiptoes to open the door and bowed again for her to enter; she smiled at him as she entered the trailer. Mr. McNamara was seated at his desk with his back to the door. Mary took in her surroundings, the wagon was cozy, and she realized why the little man had called it a palace, the small windows had royal purple velvet curtains tied back with gold tasseled ropes. The two occasional chairs were of the same material and the little sofa and Mr. McNamara's large high-backed swivel chair were covered in a beautiful tapestry material, deep blues, and the same royal purple with deep ruby red and gold piping. The large mahogany desk backed up to a paneled wall that had a painting of a court jester in many colors that were repeated in the room. The other walls were covered with framed photos of the Circus acts of both the past and present. A drape of the purple material covered a doorway, which Mary expected led to the bedchambers. The distinguished looking man with his white wavy hair turned to face her.

"Peg my little man, who have you brought to me?" He appraised Mary with his steely eyes that suddenly turned kind.

"Mr. McNamara, this young lady is looking for a job with our wonderful Circus!" He answered enthusiastically.

"And what would be your name, lass?" He asked with flare.

"Mary Eden, Mr. McNamara." She answered carefully.

"And what kind of jobs are you looking for?"

"I was hoping to be an elephant rider." She paused.

"You want to be an elephant rider?" He contemplated her request. "Well, lass that is a job most of our girls have to work up to. Most people start out working at the concessions."

Not to be put off, Mary continued, "Mr. McNamara, I would probably be good at the concessions, but I did have my heart set on being an elephant rider. I have spent summers at my grandparent's farm in Mississippi and I can ride a horse and I have a natural ability with animals."

Her enthusiasm as she spoke was noticed. Mac looked her over and decided she would look good in the costume. She had a sweet look, but also a regal air about her. She carried herself well, a trait she had inherited from Ada.

"Peg, my friend," His mind already made up he asked the little dwarf anyway, "What do you think? You are a good judge of character with your sixth sense and all."

Indeed, the little people of the circus, most of them clowns or tumblers, were noted for their perceptive powers, many had been with bands of gypsies before joining the big top.

"I have no doubts whatsoever this young lady can do anything she sets her mind to do, and I think it would be a waste of good talent to make her start at the concessions. Anyone can see that she will make the costume look good!" Peg giggled as he said this last remark.

"Then it's settled! We're leaving very early in the morning so you'd better get your things together and be ready to leave by 5 a.m."

Mary thanked him politely and left the wagon with Peg following.

"Thank you, Peg!" She said. "By the way, Peg is kind of a funny name, is it short for something else?"

"No, not really; my real name is Luigi Americas Rohos; my parents were gypsies of mixed up descent. My friends call me Peg because they think I look like a peg you would put in a hole, not very flattering, but not meant to be cruel, either. It has stuck and it is sure easier than my real name."

"O.K., Peg, I'd like to be your friend, too. I have to go now, my friend must be wondering where I got off to." She waved goodbye and hurried back to the tent and her seat next to Gail. She stayed through the final performance with Gail, not explaining her extended absence. Gail was so absorbed in the fantastic show that she hadn't even noticed how long her friend had been gone.

That night when everyone had gone to sleep, she got out of bed and packed her carpet bag with the few toiletries she had, her pretty dress, a pair of farm jeans and a plaid flannel shirt, a pair of work shoes and a pair of Sunday shoes.

She wrote a letter to Ada and told her what she was doing and asked her to forgive her. She promised to write to her as soon as she could and asked her not to worry. She ended her letter with how much she loved everyone and how much she would miss them. With that done, she left.

She sneaked out the back door at dawn and made her way quickly to the Circus grounds. She arrived on a hill overlooking the camp to see that mostly everything was torn down and ready to go. The rays of the rising sun filtered through the heavy humid dust caused by all of the workers that were scurrying around, gave the scene an eerie feeling. She stopped and looked at the anxious activity, all of the strange people she would be encountering and the unknown ahead left her feeling sick to her stomach. She dropped her bag, shut her eyes, and clutched her stomach. She bent to her knees and cried. 'What am I doing? I can't go; I've never been away from my home and family.' She looked back the way she had come from and imagined Ada in the kitchen reading her letter and crying. She sobbed, 'I have to go, and God help me! Help Ada and Little Dewey, too! I'll make it up to them as soon as I can.' She felt like a traitor, she knew Ada would be heart-broken.

Now resolved, she stifled her sobs, drew in a deep breath and dried her eyes. She took her mirror out of her purse and powdered her nose. The no longer frightened Mary stood up, picked up her bag, squared her shoulders and headed off toward the uncertain future that awaited her.

She recognized Mr. McNamara's wagon at the back of the unusual procession being prepared to leave for the train depot. She knocked then entered when she received a

"Come on in."

"Well, if it isn't little Mary, right on time, my new elephant rider. I'm glad to see you made it. Are you ready to go to work?" He was glad to see her; many had inquired before and not had the courage to leave home when the time came.

"I'm ready Mr. McNamara, what am I to do?"

"First of all, find Peg. He will get you orientated and show you where to bunk. He is my right hand man in these matters; he'll take good care of you."

It wasn't easy but she did find Peg, and he took her to the costume trailer and gave her different costumes to try on. He asked her to come out and show him each one, as he would help her decide on the one she would wear. The one they decided looked best on her was a dark green satin trimmed in gold. The top was midriff with two inch gold fringe. Around her waist was a velvet sash in a rose shade, the skirt was cut short in the front to expose her shapely legs and draped long in the back with the same gold fringe. She wore green satin tap pants under the skirt and green ballet slippers trimmed in gold.

The headdress fitted close to her head covered with gold sequins and sprouted large ostrich feathers of rose and dark green. Her hair curled from under the headdress to her shoulders. She did look quite regal.

The scene they created did not go unnoticed, leaning against a telephone pole, Demetrius observed the unintended show.

"A good choice," he said when he finally spoke and strolled over to them. "You look lovely, are you going to be our new elephant rider? Let me introduce myself, I am Demetrius Cossack, I am one of the famous Cossack Flying Trapeze artists and I would like to make your acquaintance." He took her hand and pressed his lips to the back, in the European manner, something Mary had never witnessed before, but read about, and felt flattered. She was looking at him, and he was very darkly handsome, but his arrogance spoke volumes.

"I may be pleased to make your acquaintance, I can't tell yet. I'm Mary Eden and I will be one of the famous Elephant Riders." She answered with a sheepish grin on her face.

Peg laughed. "Looks like you may have met your match, Demetrius. We have a spunky one here."

"We'll see," was Demetrius' comment.

Once the costume was decided, Mary was led by Peg through a tour of the camp. He pointed out the cages of Lions, the trailers of the performers, the elephants, where they paused, and Mary said "Which one will be mine?"

He said, "That would have to be determined by Mac, but Bingo is available," and he pointed to a very large elephant, the elephant eyed Mary and there was an instant recognition between them. She said she would like it if it was Bingo.

He said, "It's hard to get an image of what everything will be like now that we have broke it all up, but it will be wonderful."

"I saw most of it yesterday when I was here and I can't wait to see it all set up again."

"OK, well then, I will take you to your new home."

Mary was led to a wagon trailer that was to be her new home. She was introduced to the three women who she was going to be sharing the trailer with. Two were pony riders and one an elephant rider like she would soon be. The two pony riders were younger women about Mary's age. One a striking Spanish looking girl, slim, with black wavy hair down to her waist her name was Rosie. The other an innocent looking redhead with a mass of wild curls and big green eyes, a little on the plump side, she was called Debbie. The other elephant rider was a blonde woman older than the other two girls, clearly in her thirties. Her hair was straight and long and her bangs came almost to her eyes, which were hard, a cold clear blue. She was stocky but full and firm. Her name was Madelyn, but everyone called her Mad, and she said she deserved the nickname, and no one should fool with her, and she wasn't impressed with cute.

Mad pointed to the empty bottom bunk and said that was where Mary was to park herself and her stuff should go on a shelf on the opposite wall. Mad was clearly the one in charge in the tiny trailer.

Slightly intimidated, Mary parked herself and her stuff, and then asked, "Where are we going next?"

"Dallas is our next stop, one of our biggest shows, we will arrive some time tonight and have one day to set up. Our first show will be two o'clock day after tomorrow. We have two shows a day for a week, and by the time we are thru there you will know what Circus life is all about," she paused for effect, "we usually lose a couple of greenhorn cutie pies after a week of what we go through."

"Well, I'm looking forward to it." Mary answered sheepishly.

"Humph." Mad remarked.

Rosie leaned over the side of the bunk and whispered to Mary, "She's really not as bad as she wants everyone to think she is, don't be frightened. We'll get along fine."

The train was ready to roll and everyone settled down to get much needed rest, sometimes this was the best rest they would receive.

Mary was exhausted, she had not slept well the night before in anticipation of the step she was taking, and she fell into a restless sleep, dreaming about dwarfs, and big mean looking blondes, and the leering smile of Demetrius.

They arrived late that night at the Dallas fairgrounds and were allowed to sleep till dawn when everyone was roused to get busy working on setting up the big top and the concessions. The animal handlers had their jobs but the girls were expected to feed and care for the animals too so that the animals would be familiar with their riders.

Mary was introduced to her big Bingo and was taught how to mount him, she was surprised when she saw how big he was and how easy it was to get on board when he came down to his knees to accommodate her. It was exciting, all that was going on. Many of the performers were practicing their acts, and Mary was impressed again with the talents of these unusual people.

Everyone worked until sunset and some beyond. Most took their meals together on makeshift picnic tables served from the caterer's wagon; others took their meals back to their wagon to eat alone. Peg took Mary around during mealtime and introduced her to most of the rest of the crew. Everyone greeted her happily and offered her good luck with the elephants and said they hoped to see more of her. The ones missing were conspicuous with their absence, as if they were too good to eat with the others. Mary noticed Demetrius was not there. Peg introduced her to the Preacher, someone who would become an important part of her time in the Circus. He later told her the story that had circled around the camp of why the Preacher was there.

His name was Clifton Prior, and as always, acquired a nick name which to Cliff was just Preacher, he had been a Pastor of a little white clapboard church in West Virginia, his little church was growing and he was much loved. He had a pretty wife and two small children. His sermons were heartfelt and many were lead to the Lord. It was often said he was a blessed man. There was a family who attended the church, a farmer, his wife and two teenage daughters. One of the daughters took a liking to the preacher, who was handsome in a kind of tall lanky way. The young girl was a raven haired beauty named Ray Lynn; she had developed early, but still had pretty freckles across her nose. Her Daddy has chased her across the hill of West Virginia trying to keep her out of trouble.

He had asked the Pastor to talk to the girl, maybe he could help, and well, Ray Lynn had other ideas and devilishly seduced the preacher into an affair. When the Daddy found out about it, from the boys who had chased Ray Lynn without success, he called a meeting with the elders and the preacher was run out of town. His father took over the pastorship of the little church and the preacher's wife and two kids moved in with him.

As the time for the first show approached the frenzy increased, nerves were on edge. Madelyn became a real bear, the four girls trying to prepare for the show in the tiny trailer was too much for her. She snapped at Mary and the others, this is when the other three took the little table outside to put their makeup on and left her to her own.

Everything came off as was expected and the whole week in Dallas was a good show, the big top was packed every show and the concessionaires said it was the biggest take they had ever had. When the week was over Mac called everyone together and congratulated them on a job well done. Peg nudged Mary and said he was proud of her, she had taken to the routine quickly and he said she was fabulous on and around the elephants. She said she loved it. Demetrius was standing in front of them and he turned and spoke to Peg, but his eyes were on Mary.

"I see you have taken the new little farm girl under your wing, Peg."

Mary answered for him, "I am not a farm girl, Demetrius. I did spend some time on my grandparent's farm in Mississippi but I am from a small town and consider myself more of a city girl."

"Oh, a city girl or maybe a Southern Belle, maybe that farm in Mississippi was a Southern Plantation, that's more what you act like."

"Not quite, and I don't know what you mean." She answered.

"Well, you're not exactly friendly; maybe you think you are too good for the rest of us."

He was starting to get her excited and embarrassed, she felt he was trying to push her buttons.

"That's not true; I like everyone I have met so far. You are the only one who acts high and mighty."

"Prove it then, have dinner with me in my trailer."

"You've got to be kidding." Mary answered him indignantly.

"I'm not kidding, tomorrow night at seven, I'll be expecting you. Wear something special." He walked off before Mary had the chance to answer him. She stamped her foot and dust rose nearly to Peg's face.

"That jerk has a lot of nerve!" She said. She was red in the face with anger.

Peg clapped his hands together and did a little dance laughing at them. "You two are a pair; if you keep antagonizing him you will just arouse his interest more. He has been seeing Rosie, but he has been losing interest in her lately, and everyone was wondering who he would be after next, looks like it's you."

"Well, I am not interested in that arrogant sleezeball."

"More power to you, my love, but Demetrius usually gets his way."

"Not this time, I assure you. If he thinks I'll have dinner with him in his trailer," she took a deep breath, "he's as crazy as I think he is."

Demetrius interest was aroused. He hadn't had a challenge in a long time and he liked the girl's spirit and her freshness. He wasn't sure she would come to dinner and that made him more determined. He went to a lot of trouble for her just in case she couldn't resist his charms. He had the cook prepare a special dinner for two and bring it to his trailer. He tipped him well. He dressed carefully in tight black pants that showed off his muscular legs and a crisp white shirt open down the front revealing the muscles of his chest. He surveyed himself in the mirror and complimented himself on his rakish good looks. She'll show up.

By eight o'clock, she hadn't arrived and he was steaming. He stormed out of the trailer and headed to Mary's wagon. He knocked on the door and when it was opened he asked for Rosie. When Rosie appeared he grabbed her by the hand and dragged her back to his trailer. She didn't resist. He took his lust with her and she didn't mind; she wasn't the one who was losing interest and his actions made her believe he had come back to her.

She stayed the night with Demetrius and when she returned the next morning she looked happy, although he had scooted her out before she was ready to leave.

Mary often ran into the preacher, his unhappy face troubled her. She asked him if there was anything wrong. "Why do you always look so unhappy?"

"For you Mary I do have a smile." and he did smile. "Have you been to any of my church services?"

"Oh yes, going to church has always been an important part of my life. I have a lot to pray about."

"You Mary, you seem so happy all of the time."

"Well Preacher, I do have a lot to be thankful for. I always thank God for his blessing, but I worry about my family, and if I did the right thing in leaving them."

"God's ways are not always clear to us. But I am sure things will work out for you. Just keep Praying, and just call me Cliff."

"Oh I couldn't"

"Well how about Pastor Cliff?"

"OK that will work" Mary had a genuine soft spot for the seemingly sad Preacher and often looked for him to sit next to at lunch.

Mary had attended the services in the little tent with the few benches used as pews. The sermons the preacher taught were not like the ones she had grown up with. At home in the Southern Baptist church, the Pastor had always ranted and raved of hell and damnation, and pounded on the pulpit while sweat dripped off his brow, the ever present handkerchief dabbing at his face. When he was through the choir sang the beautiful songs Mary and Ada loved and that was the best part of it all for Mary. This preacher' sermons were always of God's love and Grace and promises of eternal life through our Lord Jesus Christ and his sacrifice on the Cross. Although his deliverance was bland it did touch Mary.

'God is a God of Love.' She thought. Then the preacher would sit at his Piano and seem to offer a prayer to God before he started playing. Then he would begin playing softly then he would sing and he shut his eyes as tears rolled down his cheeks. Then the spirit of the Lord descended over the few who had gathered. He played songs to Jesus that was so beautiful to hear. He sang of Grace and Mercy and Love and Heaven, where God waited and no would be alone. His voice was deep and soulful, his command of the piano unsurpassed. He trilled the keys, his deep voice would rise and touch the highest notes and his piano would keep up with him to the end of the song with sound so stunning most of the people who were gathered there, and the ones who had wonderer in while he was playing, were weeping.

They later remarked that is seemed that angels were accompanying him. When he was finished he wiped his eyes on his shirt sleeve picked up his Bible and left the church leaving all those that were there in spiritual shock.

Sometimes at night when everyone else had retired, the Preacher would go to the little tent with a half full tumbler of whiskey and a candle which he placed on top of the old upright piano. And he would play for himself. The sound carried on the quiet night, and through the camp many whispered 'There goes the preacher again,' but no one complained. The music so wonderful often worked on the crew as lullabies and they would drift off to the sleep murmuring the words to the songs the preacher was playing. Sometimes when the preacher was not playing and the crew had a hard time sleeping they would whisper among each other, 'where is the Preacher tonight.'

Mary tried to avoid Demetrius as much as possible the next couple of months. The tour was going well and the work was hard. She collapsed in her small bunk every night to an exhausted sleep. They had at least one afternoon and one evening off in each big city they went to, and the girls spent the afternoons shopping and the evenings at the movies or dining out. Everyone loved the movies, Clark Gable, Cary Grant and Errol Flynn, they all agreed, was their favorite heartthrobs. They saw Casablanca and speculated that Humphrey

Bogart would be a big star and the movie would probably get an Academy Award.

They were still talking about *Gone with the Wind* and hoped they would get to see it somewhere on the tour as Mary had not seen it yet. She had not been allowed to go to the movies, it being against her family religion and although her father did not follow any rules, Ada made the children abide by them, until they left home that is. They talked about how they would love to go to Hollywood. It all seemed so romantic.

Rosie was happy Demetrius had been spending time with her again, his pride, almost irreparably broken, he had left Mary alone, but when she saw him he would look her with sideways glances that sent chills down her spine.

They traveled to many big and little cities, and the tour promised to be the biggest they had ever had. With the war raging on all fronts, people were using the distraction and entertainment of the Circus to keep their minds off the fact that many had husbands and sons fighting in unknown places and that they may never see them again.

Chapter 8

Mary used what little spare time she had in her wagon writing and reading letters to and from home. Ada had been heartbroken and had not returned Mary's letters at first, but she had relented and wished her well and hoped she would quit soon and come back home. They had specified post office boxes across the country where they could receive their mail, picked up by Timothy, the ringmaster, while in town with Mac.

The mail was dispersed at mail call and sometimes there would be many letters from Ada which had arrived before them at the designated places. These letters often brought tears to Mary and renewed her homesickness.

During the time she spent with the animals she had made friends with Charles, the fair and handsome lion tamer. His hair was blonde, almost white and he wore it long like the mane of the lions. Sometimes when he was working with the lions, his hair seemed to rise and form a halo around his strong face. His powerful body always displayed in the tight fitting and colorful costumes and the fierceness of the whip as it slashed out and cracked at the lions, gave him the appearance and mystic of a Viking Warrior. But he was not a fierce man; he was a very kind man with a wonderful way with the animals. He confided in Mary his love for Sasha, Demetrius sister, and how Boris and Katrina, Sasha mother and father, had forbidden their relationship. She told him of her home and family and even about her marriage to Luke.

Charles was understanding and protective towards Mary and warned her about Demetrius, many had noticed his interest in Mary. Many had gossiped about the incident of the night of the dinner and how she rejected him.

Demetrius had tried to forget about Mary but could not. He in his young and famous life had not been treated like this before. He decided he would get his revenge and have fun doing it. He knew he would have to take a different approach, he realized Mary and Rosie were friends and that Mary would not have anything to do with him if he continued his relationship with Rosie. He used a worthless excuse to get into a fight with her and told her it was over between them. It was late at night, a night the other women in the wagon had not expected Rosie to return as she sometimes spent the nights with Demetrius.

She returned in tears and her Latin temper took over and she started throwing things around and cursing in Spanish until Madelyn could restrain her and she collapsed on Mary's bunk to cry herself to sleep. She was truly in love with Demetrius and moped around for several days until she noticed the interest of one of the tight rope walkers, which she started to return all in an effort to make Demetrius jealous.

Demetrius started to take meals with the rest of the crew and Rosie thought it was because he wanted to make up to her, but it was part of his plan to be closer to Mary. He was even kind to Rosie when he spoke to her and showed a friendlier attitude to all. He smiled a lot and tried to be helpful and everyone was amazed but leery of the apparent transformation of the often unruly and bad boy of the group.

He came by the tables often and smiled and said his hellos to Mary and the others there. Each exchanged glances and raised eyebrows in wonder at his good humor. 'It won't last,' was the common belief. But Demetrius was determined and his displays and gestures of good will soon laid everyone fears of his deviousness to rest, and they started to return his smiles and hellos and even patted him on the back and shook his hand in response.

Peg was one he had not fooled. His sixth sense told him that it was part of a grand plan and he continued to warn Mary about Demetrius, he told her that he could not be trusted. Mary on the other hand was beginning to soften and said to Peg to notice that he had not bothered her and seemed to have lost interest in her altogether.

He came by the stables one morning when she was feeding Bingo and giving him her good morning pat which he responded to with a hug around her waist with his trunk.

"Well, it seems you have charmed Bingo as you have everyone else in the Circus. How are you this lovely day?"

Mary looked him in the eyes and didn't see the usual arrogance in his remark. She responded with a little embarrassed laugh. "I'm fine, how are you? And what brings you to the lowly stables?"

"I hope I don't detect sarcasm in that remark. I really came to apologize for my rudeness of the past."

"Well, you do surprise me."

"I mean it, I am sorry, and I would like to make it up to you. Will you have lunch with me, I mean, well, could I sit with you at lunch today? Please find it in your heart to forgive me."

"I guess I could. Do you think Rosie would be jealous?" She asked.

"She shouldn't be; that has been over a long time now."

She had lunch with Demetrius at the picnic tables with the rest of the crew and she had a good time. He was charming and had everyone laughing and enjoying his company. 'He really could be a nice person if he tried.' She thought.

He then assumed his place next to Mary at most mealtimes and stopped by the stables every chance he got. He was taking a seemingly casual interest in her and she was accepting it. The first time he took her hand as they walked down the runway after lunch she did not refuse it. The next night they were to be in a town and he asked her to the movies and she accepted his invitation.

She was receiving a cold shoulder from Rosie, which bothered her but she felt Demetrius attentions were innocent enough and that Rosie was being silly.

They went to the movies and Demetrius was a perfect gentleman, he escorted her to her wagon after the show was over with his arm around her shoulder, he stopped short of their destination in the shadow of a big oak tree, the only light coming from the tiny windows of the wagons parked closely together. He took her into his arms and tried to kiss her. She withdrew.

"Demetrius, please, don't spoil things; we have had a nice evening."

He ignored her plea and pressed his lips hard on hers. He ground his hip into her; she was pressed up against the tree and could feel the rough bark on her back. She placed her hands on his shoulders and pushed him hard. He stumbled backwards, but recovered quickly. She noticed an angry look in his eyes, which he quickly disguised.

"Mary, I am sorry, please forgive me, I just got out of control, I'm sorry." He repeated.

"You're sorry. I'm sorry. I'm sorry I trusted you because you haven't changed Demetrius. I don't know how I ever thought you had." She stumbled her way to the door of the tiny wagon leaving him standing in the dark shadow of the big oak tree, the lights from the windows of the wagon played tricks on his face. She turned and noticed the angry sneer he had on his face, distorted grotesquely by the shimmering lights. She experienced a chill as she entered the wagon.

The next evening's show was as grand as the rest of the tour. The big top was filled to capacity and the excitement of the crowd was catching. Through each act the momentum was building to a fever pitch, the cheers were louder and people were standing and applauding. It was as if these people felt they were to see something they had never seen before. And for many, they never had. Mary's ride completed, she dismounted Bingo and donned her dark green satin cape with the rose velvet lining and joined the other performers behind the curtains to watch the rest of the show.

When it was time for Charles and his Lions to perform the Ring Master blew his silver whistle and called for silence. An immediate hush came over the audience and only soft whispers could be detected. The drum roll started and rose till the rafters seemed to vibrate. Cheers went up for Charles when he entered the ring. He was wearing a white shirt with billowy sleeves with a tight leather vest beaded and spangled in many colors. His pants were white and clung to his strong legs like a ballet dancer's. He took his bows and entered the cage where the lions were waiting and silence descended again. Again the anticipated drum roll shook the arena.

He snapped his whip and the lions obeyed his commands and climbed onto the platforms one at a time as they were directed to do. They were majestic, their backs' rippled, and their hair stood on end as they rolled their heads around, whipping their manes. They opened their carnivorous mouths, large yellow teeth gleaming, and roared frighteningly sending cheers once again through the crowd.

Charles stood with his back to Herod, one of the oldest and often cantankerous Lions. He took a flamboyant bow, as he stood upright Herod took a large swipe at his head knocking him face down on the straw covered ground. A claw opened the back of his vest and sent scarlet blood flowing down his back. Charles was stunned, but only took a minute to recover and rolled on his back. He could feel a stinging from the cut in his back but he knew he had to act fast. The lion was flying from the platform preparing to land directly on top of Charles. He rolled three times and came to his feet still holding the whip in his hand. The crowd went crazy. The Ring Master blew his whistle once, twice, four times and called the Clowns. "Send in the clowns." He yelled frantically.

Mary had been standing with Sasha, they gasped and screamed and held onto each other as the ever-ready clowns rushed past them to perform loudly and distract the crowd. Charles' two assistants had entered the cage with whips and guns to control the other lions, as it is common when another lion acts up the others usually follow suit.

The lion landed on the empty space where Charles had been, turned quickly and faced Charles prepared to make another assault. Charles had pulled his gun, and hoped he wouldn't have to use it. He never had before. He snapped his whip and commanded Herod to stay. The lion roared and leaned back on his hind legs as if to make a plunge.

Charles cracked the whip three more times in succession flicking him once on the nose and twice on the hip. Herod roared again, but instead of attacking he sat on his hind legs, his front legs flailed around in the air as he rolled his head around and let out a quiet roar. It was almost as if the lion was saying 'If I wasn't so tired and old I would have got you.'

As long as Charles had had Herod he had not acted up this way. Charles felt that it was probably the excitement of this evening and the expectations of the crowd that would make an old lion think he had to show everyone he wasn't completely tame.

Charles took a few deep breaths. He could feel the blood dripping and sticky on his back. He backed out of the cage leaving the two assistants and the other animal handlers who had entered the cage to handle the Lions who had-thank God-remained on their platforms despite their being excited and agitated.

Doc Cumin, a medical doctor who traveled with the circus and also performed in the circus doubling as a clown was waiting for Charles with Mary and Sasha as well as the other anxious performers. He had a chair waiting and told Charles to remove his vest and shirt and sit straddling the chair backwards. Sasha, who had been shaking violently, ran to Charles and threw her arms around him, he bent to receive the kiss her upturned lips offered, she would have done this whether or not her parents were watching. They were.

Boris called to her and demanded she stop making a spectacle of herself. Even at a time like this they could not forget their animosity toward Charles. Charles had the reputation of the womanizer before the Cossacks had joined the circus and when he had first laid eyes on Sasha he had forgotten all other women and dreamed only of Sasha. Demetrius had taken over his position of the bad boy of the circus community. Katrina grabbed Boris' arm as he moved to approach Sasha and Charles, stopping him. He glared at her.

Doc gently disengaged Sasha reminding her that Charles needed medical attention as well as emotional attention.

Charles removed his vest and shirt and seated himself in the straddled position on the chair. He was weak in the knees and visibly shaken, his usually tanned complexion had paled. He reached out to take Sasha hand which she took as she smiled lovingly at him.

Doc examined the wound and cleaned it with antiseptic soaked swabs; Charles winced at the sting from the medicine and Sasha grimaced for him also. Mary had taken the blood stained shirt and vest from Charles and was standing watching the Doctor intently administering his care to Charles. The Doctor stood up from where he had been sitting in a chair opposite of Charles' back and announced to everyone that Charles was going to be alright. The gash was not deep and would not even require stitches. He said that Charles had been very lucky, the thick fabric and the sequins and beads of the vest had taken all the force of the blow.

Mary took the vest and looked at it now, it was totally destroyed. She realized how lucky Charles had been. He could have been wounded badly from that one swipe of the lion's claw. The doctor sat down and applied an antibiotic swab and butter-flied the wound with tape and swabs that he carried in his black doctor's bag. Everyone had been scared for Charles and now seeing that he was going to be alright, cheers went up from the friends and enemies that gathered around Charles. Mary and Peg went to Charles and congratulated him on his bravery and swiftness, each with a hug. Sasha was able to give him another passionate kiss before being dragged off roughly by Boris, with Katrina following behind.

Mary and Peg escorted Charles down the midway to his wagon, he assured them that he would be alright now, and he just needed a rest and a shot of bourbon. They left him to his rest and Peg offered to accompany Mary to her wagon but she said she would like to say goodnight to Bingo before retiring.

Mary walked alone down the now almost empty midway. The Big Top had been orderly cleared of the anxious crowd and the only people left on the lot were the Circus crew preparing to put the show to bed. As she passed the empty concessions a figure emerged from the shadows between one concession and the other. As he approached she recognized it to be Demetrius. He came at her quickly and grabbed her hand. She was startled. He appeared to be agitated and had a wild look in his eyes.

"I have been waiting for you, I thought you would be going to the stables tonight and I wanted to talk to you." He said as he held her hand tightly.

"Demetrius, we don't have anything to talk about. I'm tired." She sighed. "It has been a long tiring night and I just want to see Bingo and go to bed." She tried to loosen his hold on her hand but he held tightly. "I have to go, Demetrius. Let go of my hand." She said angrily and yanked her hand loose, turning her back to him to head toward the stable tents.

Peg had witnessed the exchange between Mary and Demetrius. He had respected Mary's wishes of not being escorted home, as he thought she had wanted to be alone but in second thought he had a bad feeling and had decided to follow her, staying at a far distance so as not to be conspicuous. He now saw Mary enter the stables and Demetrius follow her inside, he saw Demetrius rushing at her and reaching out for her. Peg was really worried now and decided to go and get Charles because he knew if Mary was in trouble Charles would want to help and Peg could not handle Demetrius alone. He took off running as fast as he could on his short stocky legs.

As Mary entered the tent she felt a hand grab the back of her cape pulling it back roughly. The ties holding it around her neck cut deeply into her windpipe; she struggled to get her fingers between the ties and her now restricted neck. The pressure was released and a hand came over her mouth and an arm around her waist picking her up and dragging her into a dark corner where straw was stacked and strewn around. She was twisted around and tossed on the ground and Demetrius threw his body on hers. His strong legs straddled her waist and with one hand he pinned her hands together and with the other he still held her mouth.

She was struggling wildly, trying to scream, but was only able to whimper and flay her legs. There was no one in the stable tent to hear or witness her struggle. She was watching him and pleading with him with her wide, fearful eyes. She was truly scared.

Peg arrived at Charles' wagon and banged loudly. There was no answer, he tried the door and found it unlocked, not to waste time knocking again he entered the wagon. He found Charles sprawled on his bed face down with the bottle of bourbon on the floor beside the bed. He was naked to the waist only his bandages crossed his tanned back. He was still wearing the white blood stained pants he had worn that night but he had removed his shoes. Peg thought, 'I hope you haven't consumed a lot of that bourbon.' He touched Charles' shoulder and gently shook him; he awoke with a start and grimaced at the pain.

"What's going on?" He sat upright on the bed and tried to wipe the sleep out of his eyes. He recognized Peg and the strange look in his eyes. "Is something the matter?" He asked.

"I hope you are feeling better and have not drunk a lot of that bourbon." Peg answered.

"I'm okay, just a little sore, the bourbon helped but I didn't drink too much of it, what brings you back here?" He asked again.

"It's Mary. I think she is in trouble," trying to explain he became excited and started to stutter. "Dem, Dem, Demit, Demetrius. He has her."

"Calm down. What do you mean Demetrius has her?"

"I, I, I saw him follow her into the stable tent and I, I, I'm, I'm afraid he is going to hurt her."

"Okay, let's go. I'll kill that bastard if he hurts her." Charles threw on his cape and sandals and followed Peg quickly down the midway toward the stable tent.

"I don't want to hurt you, Mary, but I will if I have to. I'm tired of your high and mighty attitude. You think you are too good for me, well, I'll show you." He hissed in her face.

He removed his hand from over her mouth and replaced it with his mouth pressing hard. His tongue probed and Mary opened her mouth to receive his tongue. She had a moment of arousal and returned his kiss, she was a sensual woman and the year of frustrating marriage to Luke had been hard and left her with yearnings yet to be fulfilled. She was enjoying the kiss but soon realized who it was and what he was trying to do to her. She gasped with revulsion and felt like she would throw up. Her teeth came down hard on his tongue. She tasted blood. He reared back and slapped her hard across the face, momentarily stunning her.

He took the opportunity to unzip his trousers and pull down her tap pants. He placed a knee between her legs and spread them. She recovered from the blow and one hand loose she swiped at his face leaving welts from her fingernails on his cheek. He grabbed her hand and wrenched it under her back and placed his body hard on hers and his mouth on hers so she could not scream. He violated her.

She heard Bingo trumped and the rest of the elephants joined in. Her arm under her was throbbing and she now tasted her own blood as his teeth ground into her lips.

He was violently yanked from her. Charles and Peg had entered and found them in the struggle. Charles grabbed him by the hair and pulled him back as he planted a fist squarely on his jaw causing him to land on his rump in the corner.

Peg went to Mary who had sat up quickly and brought her cape around to cover herself up. She grabbed Peg and sobbed into his shoulder. Charles went to Demetrius and picked him up by both shoulders and threw him face down out of the opening of the tent. He scrambled to his feet, zipped and buttoned his pants and dusted himself off. Charles ran to him and threw a punch that sent him flying back to the ground. Demetrius felt blood flowing from his nose as he scrambled to his feet.

"You get out of here before I kill you, Demetrius. You're scum and you *will* pay for this." Charles' rage was evident; his face was red with anger. He was shaking again and the wound on his back had started to bleed again. He went to Mary and when Peg had risen he bent and picked her up, ignoring his own bleeding back and carried her to her wagon leaving her with the women she shared quarters with and Peg. He went to fetch the doctor for her and himself.

On the way back to the wagon, Mary, ashamed and feeling used, had pleaded with Peg and Charles not to tell anyone about what had happened. They had reluctantly agreed but said she would have to have the doctor look at her and beyond that they would try to keep it under wraps.

Peg had pulled the covers down and Charles had laid her on the bunk and covered her up before he left. Peg pulled up a chair and sat by her and took her hand. Madelyn and Rosie being concerned asked what had happened. Mary turned her head to her wall and started crying again. Peg answered that she had had a bad fall. They asked if she had fallen from Bingo and he said no. He turned from them with no further explanations, leaving the women to speculate on their own.

Being left alone Mary experienced such shame, revulsion, and guilt. She didn't know whether or not she had done anything to encourage Demetrius. She felt she probably had and therefore felt shame and guilt. She knew she had almost gotten carried away with the passion even though it was brutal and this made her feel terribly ashamed. She finally slept but whimpered and tossed most of the night.

The next morning Charles came to the trailer to see how she was and she tried to put on a good face. Her arm was badly bruised and her lip was swollen; her eye was bruised slightly from where Demetrius had hit her in the face. She had tried to cover the bruises with makeup, but Charles saw the damage and he said he was going to see Demetrius and get even with him for what he had done to her. She pleaded again with him not to go to Demetrius as this would cause everyone to know what had happened, and she was too embarrassed and ashamed for anyone to know. He said she didn't have anything to be ashamed about and Demetrius deserved to pay for what he had done. It was time he learned a lesson. Mary took his hand in desperation and asked him, please, for her, not to do this. Seeing the look in her eyes now swollen with unreleased tears, he relented and promised he would let it be but he was not at all happy about it.

"Charles, there is something you can do for me, would you take me to Pastor Cliff, I mean the Preacher."

"Of Course I will..." He tried to pick her up, she said she could walk and it would be better for all if she did.

They arrived at the Preachers wagon but he was in the tent playing and they went there.

"I have to have some time alone with him Charles."

"Okay, will you be alright."

"Yes, will you come back in an hour to get me?"

"Sure I will."

Mary entered the tent and made her way over to the Preacher, He acknowledged her and stopped playing. "What is it Mary? You look awful."

"I am sorry to bother you but something has happened and I need you to pray with me."

"It would be an honor, now tell me what happened."

Mary explained the whole situation to the Preacher. He took her hands during the story and held them now.

"Mary, Mary, Mary, this is a hard one, we will have to do this together."

"Okay," Mary said.

With tears in the preacher's eyes and Mary crying softly, they both bowed their heads.

"Dear Father in Heaven." He paused for a moment. "I haven't come to you this way in a long time, but for Mary's sake do not hide thy face from me." Mary glanced up at the Preacher and saw tears now running down his cheeks. "I am not worthy, but Mary needs you. She has taken on shame and guilt and I pray to you to remove these burdens from her and adhere to your promises, that when we ask we will receive, that your Mercy is there every day anew for us. And we are forgiven through the blood of our Lord Jesus Christ who died on the cross for our sins. I ask these things in the name of thy only son, and our savior, Jesus Christ, Amen."

Mary then embraced the Preacher for a moment and said thank you and then saw that Charles was waiting for her in the passage way of the tent. "I have to go now, but I will always remember that prayer for the rest of my life and I thank you very much. I feel a lot better now."

Mary left the Preacher there at the piano and he started to play the 'Old Rugged Cross,' he was crying openly now. He thought 'how can I feel so close to you God when I am at this piano but so unsure of my self and my relationship with you at any other time.' Then as if God had spoken to him. He realized that the words he had spoken to Mary were from God and that they were for him too. He had been carrying around the same guilt and shame for over a year now. And then he offered up a prayer for himself. "My Lord Jesus, I simply ask for forgiveness for the sins I have committed and knowing you are there I accept that forgiveness now, and I promise to always remember your Mercy. I realize now I have been just going through the motions of life without the joy of your love. I will go back home and face the consequences of my sins. I Love you Lord. I love you. I will always seek thy face, and I thank you now for everything in my life, in the name of Jesus, Amen."

Later that night alone in his wagon the preacher opened the few letters he had received from home that he couldn't open before. They were wonderful words to him. 'All is forgiven and you are welcome home. Doris and the kids miss you every day and I, your father, am too old to do the preaching anymore. We need you hear.'

The preacher was never so happy and thanked God again for his promises. He knew he would leave the Circus soon and wrote a letter home that said, he was happy now, and would be home soon. He would soon have one more task to complete before he could leave the Circus.

Circus life continued as usual. The tour was on its last leg-thru Washington State, Oregon and then California. Most of the people knew what had happened: With Demetrius scratches on his cheek and swollen jaw matching Mary's injuries left no doubt. No one spoke of the event but Demetrius was shunned, usually tolerated he was now an outcast among his fellow performers.

Mary's usually bright light was somehow diminished. She moped around a lot still in the company of Peg and Charles, who tried to cheer her up. She was only waiting for the tour to get into Los Angeles so she could leave and start over again in a new environment.

The people's respect for Charles grew, his past reputation forgotten. He became the favorite among all. Boris and Katrina noticing this and with Demetrius loss of favor allowed the older Charles to court their young beautiful daughter.

On a sunny day in Redding, California, under big redwoods, Charles and Sasha were married, by the now transformed Preacher, happiness for Charles and Sasha and himself shined on his face.

Everyone was dressed in their fanciest costumes and no other wedding was as festive as this one. Even the elephants trumpeted the event. This made Mary happy and she spent a wonderful day, as everyone did, reveling in the happiness radiating from the two lovers.

Eventually Demetrius was even forgiven and accepted back in to the grace of the Circus community. A new young girl had joined the circus and he had courted her and treated her with respect. He finally seemed to be growing up.

On arrival to Los Angeles Mary announced to her friends that she would be leaving the circus. They expressed their sorrow at losing her but had seen it coming. With tearful exchanges between herself and Peg and sad goodbyes with Madelyn, Rosie and Debbie-Charles and Sasha gave her a satin pillow with the name of the circus and a picture of an Elephant on it for a souvenir. She left with her meager possessions.

After leaving her friends, during her final visit with Bingo, he had wrapped his trunk around her and lifted her off the ground, she wondered if it was true that elephants never forgot and if someday she saw him again he would remember her. He set her down and she hugged him around his front leg. With a lump in her throat she vowed to forget the bad times she had experienced and only remember the good friends she had made and all the fun the Circus had given her.

PART THREE

LIFE CONTINUES

Chapter 9

Mary gathered the remnants of her Circus life back together and placed them back in the carved Box from which she had taken them. She wondered where the satin pillow Charles and Sasha had given her had gone. She hoped they were still happy and knew that they were. She felt they would be happy for her with her new life, and Peg, she knew he would have found a new young girl to watch after. As she remembered, she knew she would not have made it through the end without those friends.

She reflected on the reason she had not told Dante the truth about what happened. She had seemed to have forgotten the whole terrible experience of the violation. Was it the shame of giving in momentarily to the kiss, or was it just easier to tell the story the way she did. Was there less shame in the way she told it? She knew that she would have to explain the whole truth of what happened to her to Dante. Would he hate her? Or would he understand?

The baby whimpered and Mary quickly went to the closet and placed the box back where it had been hidden, and entered the bedroom to quiet the baby lest she wake up Dante.

She peered into the bassinet at the still sleeping baby. 'She must have been dreaming' she thought, as a little whimper escaped again from the baby and a little smile came over her precious face. Mary marveled again at her good fortune to have found a man like Dante and have a new little baby like Anna. She crept back into the bed and placed her body in the spoon of Dante's body; he placed his arm around her and pulled her closer, still sleeping.

The next morning being Sunday they arose early and had breakfast and got dressed for church, and Sunday Dinner with Ada and Earl.

During their fried chicken dinner, they discussed the possibility of Ada and Mary and the baby, going south to visit the relatives. It was decided it would be okay with Earl and Dante if they were not gone too long. March 15th was set as a date for departure.

After everyone was settled at their homes and the baby asleep, Mary told Dante she had something to tell him. He sat down at the dining room table with Mary and prepared to listen.

"Is it bad?" he asked.

"I think so."

She told him how she lied to him about being with Demetrius, how he had forced himself on her.

He asked. "He forced himself on you?" Dante's eyes shone with fury, "Why did you lie to me?"

"I don't know, maybe I didn't remember exactly how it had happened but last night the horrible experience came back to me."

"But you lied to me."

"I didn't mean too." Dante got up quickly from his chair knocking it over as he left the room to go to his study."

Mary was shocked, she didn't know what to expect from Dante, but this seemed extreme. "Oh Dear God, what have I done? You have given me so much, how could I hurt him so?" She wailed. 'Surely now he will hate me, that pedestal he has put me on is truly shattered now,' she thought.

She went to bed alone and finally cried herself to sleep; she realized she had carried this shame and now she would have to pay for it. Dante stayed in the study and slept on the couch that was in there.

The next morning they met in the kitchen, neither one of them had slept very well.

Dante said, "Mary I am sorry I acted like that. I realize it wasn't your fault. I was just so angry at that Demo, whatever his name is, and there is nothing I can do about it now. If he was here now I would probably come close to killing him."

"Dante, can you forgive me for lying to you."

"I don't believe you meant to lie about it, it's just so frustrating I can't get my hands on him."

"You remember I told you about Charles, well, he did get in a few good punches at Demetrious, and Demetrious was shunned for quite a while."

"Good," said Dante, and he took her into his arms. And Mary was finally able to give up her shame and guilt. She thanked God in a silent prayer.

As the date approached, Ada and Mary became excited with the anticipation of a trip, not all of it good excitement, as it was mixed with the fear of returning to a place not always happy, and their nervousness showed.

"Are you sure you want to make this trip?" Dante asked one evening as they were sitting on the floor in their duplex playing with the baby.

"I really don't have a choice," she sighed and continued, "I have to admit I am frightened, but I can't forget that my Grandma is quite ill and I would like to see her before she dies. I also want to see my relatives and show off my little Anna. I only wish you could come, too." She tickled Anna under the chin and she responded with coos and baby talk.

"I understand. I wish I could come too, but you know I can't." He hesitated, "Why don't you and Ada buy some new clothes to wear for your trip."

She laughed at this "Dante, the clothes we have now will be just fine, in fact, probably too good. You have to realize these people are mostly farm folks and wear simple clothes. The clothes you have bought me and Ada are much updated and they probably haven't seen anything like them except in magazines."

"I think everything will be alright, you and Ada are a strong pair."

'I hope you are right, Dante,' she thought.

They arrived at the Greyhound Bus Station in Odessa, Texas late at night and Uncle Henry was there to meet them. Both women were very tired, the two days and one night they had spent on the bus getting to Texas had been very exhausting. Uncle Henry looked very tired, too, but greeted them with a warm Texas smile.

"Well, my, my goodness, y'all are sight for sore eyes; I have never seen a pair like you outside the movie screens. And what is that pink bundle. Come here and give your Uncle a big hug."

"Uncle Henry!" They both exclaimed in unison and one took hold of his hand and kissed it while the other gave him a hug. They parted and Mary held open the pink blanket to expose the adorable sleeping face of the little baby girl.

"Uncle Henry, she's sleeping now but I would like you to meet Anna, Maryanna..."

"Well, look at her! That black hair and those rosy cheeks! What a little doll baby, your Aunt Mabel will

129

just eat her up!" At that, little Anna yawned and opened her eyes to gaze at her great uncle.

"Look, she woke up. My! What beautiful big eyes she has." Uncle Henry was smiling at the baby. The baby answered with a big smile and her little pink tongue escaped from between her rose bud lips.

"Whoa! I think I love her already, Mary. Is she always this happy when she wakes up?"

"Well, not always but most of the time and she loves to smile at handsome men. I think she knows her charm already."

"Well, let's get going, its late and Mabel will be wondering where we are, you know what a worry wart she is. She'll have some hot tea and homemade chocolate brownies waiting for you. Then you can rest. We have a big day tomorrow; the entire family is coming over for a big dinner in honor of you three girls."

"Is Dewey going to be there, Henry?" Ada asked her brother tentatively.

"No, Ada, dear, we thought it would be best not to invite him tomorrow afternoon, but he is coming over later in the evening to see y'all. I hope that's alright." He answered.

"Well, I guess it can't be avoided. I can't tell you how much I am dreading it..." Ada was very much dreading the meeting but also very anxious in a strange way to see Dewey.

The thought of it right at this time started to make her tremble from the inside out like a volcano starting to erupt. 'You have to get a hold of yourself, you can't fall apart now in front of Mary and Henry,' she thought. She shivered and Mary noticed.

"What's the matter, Mama?" She asked with concern in her voice.

Ada had felt as if someone was walking over her grave. She wrapped her coat lapels tighter around her neck, picked up the overnight bag she had left on the floor and said, "Just a chill, we better get going as your Uncle said."

The next day, refreshed, the two women enjoyed the great dinner and the family company. Henry and Mabel's two daughters and their husbands along with their brood together of five children, and baby Anna, which everyone adored and fussed over, each child in turn wanted to hold her. The dinner consisted of the usual Southern fare, delicious country ham, collard greens and green beans-grown in the backyard garden, candied sweet potatoes that were so sweet and syrupy that they were almost chewy in consistency, mashed potatoes and cornbread. Of course, for dessert Texas Pecan Pie topped with rich whipped cream was served.

Everyone was stuffed. When finished, the women cleaned the table and did the dishes then sat around the living room talking softly while Uncle Henry dozed in his chair. The other two men were sitting on the porch smoking cigarettes, watching the children now playing in the yard. The afternoon lazed on until the two men came in from the porch about the beginning of sunset and announced it was time to go home, saying if they left now they would be home before dark. They began gathering together their women and they gathered their kids and belongings taking wrapped leftovers with them. Ada started to shake; her eyes got big and almost pleaded, "Y'all don't have to go already do you?"

She grabbed one of the women's arms alarming her. "What's the matter, Ada, you look like you seen a ghost." The cousin asked her.

Of course, Ada knew when the relatives would leave shortly thereafter Dewey Sr. would arrive. "Oh, forgive me! I am okay; I just know it will be a long time until I see y'all again." She lied.

She kissed her cousin on the cheek, still shaking. She hugged the husbands and the little ones and kissed her other cousin and genuinely felt a loss at their departure.

She sunk down on the sofa when the relatives left and held her hands in her lap until they stopped trembling, Mary came over and put her arm around her and whispered in her ear.

"Maybe we should tell Uncle Henry to call Daddy and cancel this meeting, Mama. You look scared to death."

"I am honey, but it wouldn't be fair, he does have a right to see his grandbaby, I'll get through alright, I really will." She patted Mary's hand and hugged her for reassurance.

They sat in silence holding hands until the knock on the door announced Dewey Sr.'s arrival.

Uncle Henry answered the door. "Come on in DC, Ada and Mary have been waiting for you." Mary had moved from the couch and stood behind her uncle awaiting her father's entrance into the room. Uncle Henry moved to the side to let DC enter.

Mary stared at him for a minute; he was handsome as ever. His ever-thick hair now quite gray was combed back from his clear brow; his now sad eyes welled up with tears. He had on his Sunday best suit and had removed his hat which he now held in his two hands. A tear escaped his eyes, his lip quivered as he tried to speak; he held out his arms offering Mary? She hesitated a moment too long and he started to drop his arms and lower his head. Just then she melted, a sob escaped her and she ran to him and threw her arms around him; she buried her head on his shoulder and cried.

"Oh Daddy, oh Daddy, I have missed you!"

"I have missed you, too," he paused "and your mother." He was staring at Ada on the couch, now crying, too. She was using her handkerchief and dabbing her eyes. She tried to regain her composure. She stood up, straightened her dress, dabbed her eyes again and replaced the handkerchief in her pocket.

"Hello, Dewey. You look good; I hear you have been doing well." He kept his arm around Mary possessively.

"I have been trying, I have a job and my health is good. You both look wonderful; I guess California agrees with you. Hey, where is my grandbaby?" He asked Mary.

"Daddy, you will love her! She is so cute! I'll go get her." She left the room for the bedroom where Anna had been sleeping in the middle of Henry's and Mabel's feather bed.

Dewey Sr. stood fidgeting with his hat that was still in his hands. Uncle Henry offered to take his hat and offered a chair for him to sit in opposite Ada. The thick atmosphere between the two could be cut with a knife with unspoken emotion.

Mary came back with the baby and asked if her father wanted to hold her. He said he would like that very much; it had been a very long time since he held a baby. He gazed into the baby's sleeping face, 'An angel,' he thought. He lifted her to his chest and buried his face in the soft blanket taking in the aroma of fresh sweet milk and baby powder that all well kept babies had. As he did this he hurt deep inside for the family he had lost.

Mary took the baby back to the bedroom. Mabel offered iced tea for everyone and left to prepare. Henry left to put Dewey's' hat in the hall where the hat rack stood.

Dewey Sr. asked Ada if they could go for a walk and talk a little as the night was mild and the full moon was starting to come up over the horizon. He mentioned that the skies were not the same in California like they were here in Texas. She agreed and went for her shawl, meeting Henry and Mary both in the hall. Slightly embarrassed, she explained that she and Dewey Sr. were going for a short walk and not to worry, everything would be alright.

As they descended the porch stairs Dewey Sr. took Ada's hand, she did not protest. It was a familiar and natural thing to do, two people who had shared 21 years of their lives together, whether it be good or bad. This bond would never be broken by time or circumstance.

"DC, you are right. There is not a sky in the world like the big Texas sky at night. I do miss it."

Ada spoke through the silence they had created, each choking on unspoken emotion.

"Ada, I didn't bring you out here to talk about the sky," he grabbed her by the shoulder and turned her to face him, "Ada, I love you."

She stared at him and did not answer.

"Ada, can you hear me? I love you." His grip on her shoulders tightened.

"I hear you alright, DC, but you know it is way too late now. You look good and I can tell you have been trying to straighten your life out but there is no going back."

"You look so beautiful to me right now, where did you get those clothes, they fit you so well. I always wished I could have given you the things you deserved."

"It doesn't matter where I got them, and don't concern yourself about my life now. What's done is done, right or wrong."

"It doesn't have to be."

"Yes, it does, DC, too much has happened. When you burnt the house down you took away my past and then you proceeded to ruin our future with your women and drinking, and the treatment of me and the kids. The way you treated Little Dewey, he was such a precious boy and you acted like you hated him, now he is in that terrible war."

She couldn't continue. She shook his hands off her shoulders and buried her face in her hands and began to cry softly.

He reached for her, took her face in his hands, and turned it up to face him and kissed her on the cheek and each eye in turn.

"I don't know what made me do those things. Maybe I was jealous of Dewey. Both you and Mary doted on him so and he was so ornery and always defying me."

"Stop it DC. You never understood him. He loved you. He was never ornery he only did things that boys do. With his good nature he couldn't help smiling and you took that for defiance. You broke his heart every day."

"Oh, Ada," He lamented and sighed, "I have made so many terrible mistakes and I realize that now, you have no idea how much I know that now. I have lost so much, you were always there, always kind, always such a good mother and I would drink and—"

"You would drink and then you would go and pick up women and then you would come home and terrorize our family."

"Can you ever forgive me? It's taken me a long time to get better. I tried after you left but it didn't work, the loss was too great. When I heard you had gotten married again I stopped for good and I haven't had a drink in ages. I'm a changed man, Ada, and I love you with all my heart."

"DC, I can forgive you and I can hurt for you, too. But I can never forget, and I hope you can continue to be sober and healthy and have a better life in the future."

"I can never have a life without you and the kids."

"DC, they are not kids anymore and I hope they can survive their past and have good lives. I know they have forgiven you. You can see that through Mary. You are their Daddy and always will be, but you have to go on."

"I guess that's it then, I'll leave you now. I can't go back in the house. I'm too ashamed. Remember that I loved you and Mary and Little Dewey and I'll never forget that precious little baby." He left then, disappearing into the black night. She heard the door slam and the motor start the old car he was driving.

She felt the aching loss in the pit of her stomach and a sob rose from her chest, but she caught it in her palm before it had the chance to escape from her mouth and hurried back to the house. She sat on the porch for a while.

Her emotions in a twirl, she questioned herself, 'had she done the right thing?' He certainly seemed sincere now and like his old self of many years ago before the heavy drinking began. She started to remember the good times. Oh, there was always drinking, he always had a few beers, even during the prohibition he had made his own beer, and she had never liked it but he was happy and loving and what a great lover. Something she thought she never would appreciate, but she really enjoyed with him. He was so handsome, he still is, and he was good to the children when they were wee ones.

Mary, of course, was always his favorite. She was so sweet and quiet and never bothered anyone; she guessed it was the depression, oh how everyone suffered when he got laid off. He spent days moping around the house not combing his hair or bathing, and constantly drinking. Then one morning he would get up, bathe, be happy, and get dressed to go looking for a job. When he came home he would be drunk from meeting his friends like himself who had no jobs and the cycle would start again.

The violent behavior started shortly thereafter. Little Dewey would get in his way or do something and he would knock him across the room. He took all of his anger out on him at first; a man who cannot provide for his family has a lot of anger in him. Then he would start on Ada. He would go out and when she would ask him about it he would punch her or twist her arm. Then there were the guns.

He had guns for hunting and the night he had held the gun to Little Dewey's head and threatened to kill him if any of them would move. She thought she felt that if he didn't have them his guilt would go away.

And then when he burned the house down for insurance money was the final straw. She remembered that day so vividly, like it was yesterday.

It had been a beautiful Sunday and DC had gotten up happy and suggested a picnic by the pecan orchard. They would take the old buggy for a leisurely drive and eat their Sunday dinner under the pecan trees. Then they would gather pecans so she could make her famous pecan pie for the coming Easter Sunday. He had been so animated, he had been infectious. The kids grabbed each other's hands and danced around saying 'we're going on a picnic and we're going to get pecans in the old buggy!' Ada laughed her wonderful, happy laugh that reminded you of church bells ringing until she had to have them stopped.

She was doubling over with laughter and even DC laughed at them. She asked Mary to help her in the kitchen, as there was chicken to fry and potatoes to peel for potato salad. She was glad she had made an apple pie yesterday because it would be great for desert.

'We'll make a jug of iced tea and take peaches and we have to cut up some carrots. We'll need pickles and olives. Oh, it's going to be a great day!' She had thought.

It was beautiful and warm; the sky was so purely blue. The air smelled of new blossoms and freshly grown grass from the rains of March. They were on their way down the dirt road; the trail of dust behind them was thick. They rounded the bend and DC said he had forgotten something. He explained he didn't want them to have to go back again in all that dust so he would go back on foot while they waited in the buggy and they could have the peaches while they waited. He said he'd go as fast as he could.

While they waited they ate peaches and saved one for their Daddy. They sang church songs like 'Jesus loves me this I know for the Bible tells me so, little ones to him belong, they are weak but he is strong.'

He returned out of breath with a wild look in his eyes. He grabbed the reins and made the horse go faster than before. They did have a good picnic, everyone was happy. They devoured the food and gathered many pecans, enough to give some to the favorite old lady who lived down the road who could not gather them for herself.

They returned late in the afternoon singing the church songs, even DC joined in. They smelled the smoke and wondered where it was coming from and when they rounded the familiar bend, they knew.

Dewey Sr. already knew he had done a good job. The house was no more, nothing but the fireplace stood. Many people were gathered around but the fire had already been there and left by the time they arrived. There was nothing they could do. The house had been consumed in flames. No one ever guessed Dewey Cecil Eden had burned his own house down except for Ada. She knew right away. She knew when he had left them in the buggy and had returned with that look in his eyes- which at the time had puzzled her. There was not a doubt in her mind that as sure as he was breathing he had done it.

Everything was gone. What hurt her most was losing all of the baby pictures and the books and the few toys for the kids. He collected the money and one day she told him she knew he had done it and he hit her and denied it. She would never forgive him for the horrible, mean and dishonest thing he had done.

She gazed at the full moon now high in the sky and asked God's forgiveness for herself and DC and went into the house for a restless, sleepless night.

They arose the next morning to the baby's whimpers. They had planned to stay another day but Ada said she had to leave, and as much as she would like to spend time with Henry and Mabel she had to get out of that town, there were too many memories there. Henry and Mabel said they understood and that they were happy to have spent the time they had with them.

They left for the bus station with Henry driving them. He helped them onto the bus and returned home. DC had gone to the house to see Ada one more time and had been told by Mabel that they had already left. He had driven like a madman to the bus station and parked his car and ran to where the bus was just leaving. He saw it round the bend and out of sight.

Mary had glanced out the window as the bus rounded the bend and had seen her Daddy standing there with his arms limp at his sides, she raised her hand to wave goodbye but now he was out of sight.

"Mama, he was there."

"Who was there? Who was where?"

"Daddy, Daddy was at the bus station."

"Oh."

Dewey Cecil bought a quart of Wild Turkey and returned to his little apartment now straightened up in case he had been able to bring his family there and proceeded to get rip roaring drunk.

He broke things and emptied all the cupboards on the floor, sat in the hard wooden chair and took one shoe and one sock off and placed his shotgun between his knees with the barrel in his mouth. He used his toe to pull the trigger and blew the top of his head off.

Henry had returned home and was having noontime dinner when Mabel mentioned that DC had been by to see Ada, and had left quickly when he was told that they had decided to leave early.

He finished his dinner but had a funny feeling. He went to get his coat and Mabel asked where he was going. He said he was going to check up on DC, that he had a very uneasy feeling about him.

He found him on the floor. The chair had turned over and the gun was several feet away apparently the blast had propelled him across the room. Henry, in shock and despair, cleaned the mess Dewey SR. had created in his rage and called the police. He waited for them to arrive and explained that Dewey must have been cleaning his rifle when it went off. No one but the family was ever told that he had committed suicide.

When the women arrived in Mississippi they were greeted with the horrible news and had to turn around to go back to Texas for the funeral. Ada's sister, Minnie Pearl, went with them to help with the baby. The two women were in shock with grief and guilt. Their faces were white and their eyes shone out of deep sockets with scary stares, their hands shook and their knees were weak. They leaned on each other for support. Minnie Pearl had to take the baby from Mary's arms; she was holding her too tight.

Grandma Eden came from Mississippi by car with her brother; she was a sweet tiny woman weighing no more than 90 lbs. She was part Indian and her long black hair was streaked with gray and pulled severely back from her dark scrunched face into a bun at the base of her neck. She came between the two taller grieving women at the gravesite to put her arms around both of their waists. She told them they were not to blame and that Dewey Cecil had always been a little crazy. She said it wasn't easy for a mother to admit that because he had always had such a charming way, but she had always known it nonetheless. But, she said, he was her son and she always loved him. "So I know how you both feel," was what she said to the two grieved women.

Dewey Jr. was given a week's leave and met the women in California. Mildred, his girl, came with him and they stayed at Ada and Earl's, and got married in Ada's living room before he had to return to active duty. Having him there with them was what it took to bring them out of their state of shock.

Chapter 10

1944 passed with horrible news of the war. Mary and Ada had gone to the movies and at the beginning, the newsreel's grainy black and white footage showed many horrifying images. Landing crafts, men hurrying out onto the sand, and many being shot and floating in the waves even before they could make landfall. This terrified the women and each would get down on their knees at night and pray for CL, "God, oh God, please let him be alright. He is so good, we need him so much, we love him so much, he deserves a life, please God; let him come home safe."

CL's letters were few, but he told a story of an island he had spent some time on, an island first thought to be beautiful, green, lush, mountainous, and barely touched by civilization, but had turned out to be a horrible place. It rained all the time and everything was soggy; the swamps were inhabited by giant crocodiles and spiders as big as your fists. There were tree leeches and scorpions and centipedes. By nightfall, the mosquitoes would come in clouds and their bite would bring exotic fevers. More men were dying of Malaria than enemy bullets.

In truth, his letter came from a hospital in Hawaii where he was in bed suffering from one of those exotic fevers called Elephantiasis. He would soon be discharged at this time, recovered, but not cured of the filthy disease.

He returned home with Betty who was now pregnant and starting to show. CL and Betty were to stay at Ada's and Earl's until they could get on their feet. CL was still weak and pale, he had lost a lot of weight, his face was gaunt, and his eyes were haunted.

He tried to put on a good face to everyone, but for a young man he had seen so much suffering and had experienced so much fear. He wasn't ready to talk about what he had been through and might never be. He did tell the name of the island he had been on-being Guadalcanal and that many of his friends had died and he felt lucky to be alive.

The Navy doctors told him that he might have reoccurring attacks from the disease and that if this occurred he would probably have to have surgery. CL's ever present smile was now missing.

Then there was the horrible Circus fire in Connecticut that Mary read about in the newspaper. It was the Greatest Show on Earth and 168 people died when the big top collapsed. The paper called it 'The Day the Clowns Cried,' they suspected it was a carelessly tossed cigarette and a lot of people were trampled in the panic as they tried to get out. Their passage was blocked by the animal cages and the bodies were piled 5 and 6 deep. This made Mary very sad as she thought of her time in the Circus and the friends she had made. She knew what a great tragedy this was for the people in the Circus to lose their friends and family. And to think of the people they were trying to entertain being burned.

Chapter 11

Mary and Dante settled back into a routine after all that had happened. They were enjoying Anna, doting on her, as neither one would let her cry without picking her up. It was obvious she was spoiled. Ada warned them of this but she was just as bad. They thought she was so beautiful and decided to enter her in a baby beauty pageant. It was held in the Hollywood Bowl on a bright sunny day. The biggest of the baby pageant season, and among close to 100 contestants, she was crowned Baby Queen of California.

Mary and Dante could hardly believe it. They thought that surely they had a future movie star on their hands. They had a portfolio of pictures made of their 7 month old baby and enrolled her in the Children's Screen Actors Guild. She was auditioned for a movie with

Elizabeth Taylor called 'Threes a Family' but didn't get the part because there were twins. When making a movie babies can only be used for a certain amount of time during the day and the twins could be used twice as long. Not daunted, Mary took Maryanna to other auditions only to have the same results.

Mary was now pregnant with her second child, and was not having as easy of a time as she did with Anna. She was experiencing morning sickness and being very tired in the afternoon, so Anna's movie career was temporarily put on hold. Anna was becoming a handful. She was a healthy, strong-willed twenty month old by now; getting into everything. When she wouldn't get her way she would scream and hold her breath until she would pass out and fall over on the floor. Mary now realized that what Ada had told her was right; this one was spoiled rotten. She would complain to Dante who would try to soothe her and spend more time with Anna. Part of the trouble was Mary's preoccupation with the way she was feeling, and Anna was feeling the lack of attention.

Dante spent the early evenings playing with Anna and drilling her on ABC's and nursery rhymes when Mary would be prone on the couch with exhaustion after a day of chasing after the 'little brat;' as Mary had began to call her. Anna was very smart and learned quickly. Although she didn't have a full vocabulary at 20 months old, shortly thereafter, she could recite the ABC's and several nursery rhymes.

Ada tried to help out during the day, but Betty had had her little baby girl and needed Ada's help also. Ada was running back and forth between the two households and kept very busy doing laundry, hanging the diapers out, and cooking dishes for the two families. It was good for her and she really loved it. She liked to complain once in a while but everyone knew she loved it.

Betty's baby was named, Diane, and as dark haired and eyed as Anna was, Diane was completely fair. Born bald, she soon had blonde fuzz and clear blue eyes. She was very plump and sported the family dimples.

The family Sunday dinners were now a real occasion. Ada's flower garden, now the best in the neighborhood, supplied the flowers for the church each Sunday and many bouquets for the house, which gave the house a festive feeling.

Anna, always dressed in the prettiest frilly dresses, knew how to get everyone's attention, as Dante would put on a record and she would do a wiggly dance. Then crawl into CLs' lap-he became her favorite-but Earl was not to be neglected. After kissing CL-she would run to Earl's lap and he would perform magic tricks to amuse her-he would pull out candy out of his ears and she would squeal with laughter. After dinner, when Earl would be dozing in his chair, the women would be talking, and baby Diane would be getting the attention, Dante and CL would go for a walk and take Anna with them.

She loved to walk in Grandma Ada's garden as it was so beautiful. The big pink flowering tree shaded nearly all with shadows; the petals on the walk ways reminded one of pink snow. The sun shining thru cast a warm glow. There were mosses and ferns everywhere and daisies of white and yellow. There were pansies with their velvet faces of purple, yellow and white, snap dragons of pinks and lavenders and light blues, roses, climbing and in bushes, and many unknown flowers of all colors in the garden. Anna would chase the many butterflies in the garden and go to a flower and ask Dante 'What's this one called?' and he would tell her. She would try to repeat the names and felt proud if she came close to what he had said.

Mary didn't get big with this pregnancy either. She couldn't keep much food down, but towards the end of the pregnancy she started to feel better and entered Anna in another Baby Beauty contest. She made her a little red satin bathing suit trimmed with small ruffles and silver sequins. Anna wore little white patent leather sandals. Her ever-curly chestnut colored hair, Mary had twisted into attractive ringlets. Anna won this contest and was Miss Glendale before the age of two.

She knew how to act now. When the photographers for the local newspaper asked to take her picture with her trophy and satin chest ribbon with 'Miss Glendale' on it, she pumped up her chest and threw her shoulders back and gave them her award winning smile. 'Oh, what have we created,' Mary thought.

Anna always wanted to be outside but would wander away. Mary found her one time with all her clothes off sitting on the curb playing in the water in the gutter. She got her first of many spankings that day.

A couple moved in next door with a little boy Anna's age. Mary and Dante got her a little puppy, Anna called Boots, to keep her occupied. He was a brown and white Chihuahua. She loved the puppy but the little neighbor boy and her usually fought.

They were cute together and would sometimes kiss and be best friends but Anna didn't want to share anything with him. One time he hit her over the head with a ketchup bottle and raised a bump on her forehead bigger that a walnut, and a small cut sent blood down her face. She reached up and brought her tiny hand down with the blood on it and proceeded to scream bloody murder, and then fake a faint.

Mary and Dante had become friends with the Jewish couple from New York. Nathan was tall and thin with dark hair and a beautiful prominent nose; he always wore white shirts with a tie and many different hats. He was a clown and kept them entertained. His wife, Bobbie, was small and thin, except for her rather wide hips, with hair the color of carrots. She had a bubbly personality and a laugh that could be infectious, especially when she would start to snort. Then she would start all over again- this time laughing at herself. They played cards together and enjoyed each other's company.

The incident with the ketchup bottle did cause some trouble, despite Mary's knowledge of her daughter's selfish ways. She had the natural instinct of any mother to defend her daughter. When Bobbie said that Anna probably deserved it, they went a week without talking to each other. It wasn't until Dante intervened, and asked their friends over for dinner. That all was settled now and they were friends again.

Mary and Dante's new baby was also a girl. She was full term but only weighed 4 lbs and 6 ounces. Mary had a very easy time delivering her.

She was resting quietly, waiting for the nurse to bring her the new baby for the first time, and feeling pretty good. She felt her now flat stomach and was happy it was over. She vowed she would never have any more babies. 'Two is enough, even if they are both girls' she thought.

The rotund nurse entered the hospital room carrying the tiny pink bundle, and placed the baby in Mary's outstretched arms. Mary had a big grin on her face, soon to be replaced with a frightful look as she peeled back the pink blanket and took her first look at the new baby.

"This is not my baby," she said to the startled nurse.

"What do you mean?"

"Look at her! She looks like a Mexican baby, she's so dark and," she peeled the blanket back further, "Oh My God! She's got hair all over her body!"

"Let me see, I'll check her I.D." The nurse read the I.D. and said, "It says Baby Vianney, is that your last name? What nationality is Vianney?"

"Yes, it is my last name and it's Italian. What's that got to do with anything?"

"Well, sometimes Italians are dark." The nurse was starting to get irritated with Mary. And Mary was starting to cry.

"There's some kind of mistake, where is my husband?"

Just then, Dante walked into the room. He immediately noticed Mary crying and asked, "How are my two girls?"

"There's been a mistake! Dante, this isn't my baby."

"There hasn't been a mistake, Mr. Vianney. The I.D.'s match, she is just being hysterical. It's your baby alright."

The big nurse had seen all kinds of babies: pinks, browns, reds, yellows, and blacks. She wasn't surprised at the baby in Mary's arms when she saw the dark good looks of the husband.

"Let me see her, Mary." Dante said. He was concerned. Why should he take the nurse's word over his wife's? 'A mother should know her own baby when she sees it,' he thought.

When he looked into the face of the baby he saw a whole different picture. To him, he saw a precious face, so tiny, with itty-bitty ruby lips and a button nose.

He laughed. "She's precious! I'll admit she's dark, but some of my family is darker than me. I think she's ours, Mary." He laughed again.

"She'll lighten up some and that hair will rub off fast enough," the nurse said over her shoulder as she left the room. She felt she should leave the couple alone for a while.

"Her face looks pinched," Mary lamented.

"Now, Mary, her face doesn't look pinched. She has a really cute face."

"Let me have her again." Dante placed the baby back in Mary's arms and the baby awoke, yawned, opened her clear eyes and looked right into Mary's eyes. Mary's heart melted, and she smiled.

"I guess she is our baby." She smiled at Dante.

They named the new baby Antoinette Maria Vianney. She lost a few ounces the week Mary and her spent in the hospital, and she had to stay another week in the incubator until she had reached 5 lbs. When she came home she looked much better, as her complexion had lightened up and taken on a rosy glow. She had filled out, and most of the hair on her body had rubbed off. She was a very good baby, with a sweet smile and a sweet personality. Her sparkling near-black eyes would flash when she smiled and Mary loved her dearly.

She could put her in the bassinet and leave her for hours, and Tonia would entertain herself. If anyone would come near her she would smile and wiggle her arms and legs in anticipation of company. The first day Mary brought her home she had laid her on the middle of the bed and went to the bathroom. Anna's curiosity got the best of her as she crawled on the bed, got the

baby, and was holding her on her cross-legged lap, poking her in the stomach when Mary came out of the bathroom.

"What are you doing with the baby, Anna? She is not a doll!"

"I know, Mama. I was just trying to make her make a noise." Anna had dolls that if you poked or squeezed them they would make a crying sound.

"Anna, if you keep poking her the way you are she will make plenty of noise, and you will hurt her. I don't want you to ever pick her up without permission. Do you hear me?"

"O.K., Mama." Anna started crying and pushed the baby out of her lap. Mary grabbed the baby before she could fall to the floor and Anna ran and got into her bed, screaming at the top of her lungs.

Mary put little Tonia in her bassinette and went to Anna.

"Anna, Tonia is your little sister, and she is just a little baby. You're getting to be a big girl now, you can't poke her like one of your dolls; she is very delicate."

"But, Mama, I am the baby."

"Yes, you are still a baby sometimes, but Tonia is the new baby and we all love her very much. You have to be careful not to hurt her. She will grow up like you have and be a playmate to you." Mary ruffled Anna's curls, gave her a kiss on her forehead then wiped the tears from her eyes.

"Is that okay with you?"

"I don't know yet." She smiled at her mother her irresistible sheepish smile. "Maybe, if I can play with her."

"Only if you are careful with her, I will let you feed her later today."

"O.K., I'll try to be careful," Anna said with mixed emotion.

Thus started Anna's jealousy of the new baby, but in secret she loved her too. When no one was looking she would go to Tonia and give her a gentle kiss on her soft silky cheek.

Anna grew more rambunctious and smarter every day. Tonia was adorable and now Mary and Dante had two little dolls to dress up and take out.

Chapter 12

Midred was pregnant again and getting as big as a house. Dante had gotten CL a job at Lockheed, where he had gone to work, right after he and Mary were married. Lucky for Dante, as he had received a notice to report to duty and his supervisor told him he didn't have to worry about it-as he was important to the war effort being employed by Lockheed. So, CL was doing well without any reoccurrence of the fever. He and Betty had gotten an apartment on their own in a Government housing project, on Glenoaks Boulevard, in the San Fernando Valley.

In later years, the development was to be known only as the 'Projects' as it became very run down-as many low cost housing projects do-and resembled the slums of New York. Eventually, they were torn down and a golf course was developed in their place.

Midred had another girl and called her, Delores, but she was instantly referred by all the family as Sissy.

Then Mildred proceeded to get pregnant again six weeks later.

Mary and Dante decided to take a trip back East to see Dante's family. It had been put off for so long with the involvement in Mary's family. They communicated through letters and phone calls, and many pictures back and forth of the growing families on both sides. There were now 8 grandchildren under the age of 4 years old. They decided to drive the car and make a real vacation of it, and enjoy the countryside along the way.

They planned to arrive on the day before Christmas Eve. This turned out to be a real mistake. First of all, Dante had never had to be cooped up with Anna before for more than a day. And as so goes, he had less patience than previously displayed, and Anna had no patience at all. His impatience increased with every mile and every question that never stopped coming from Anna. 'I have to go to the bathroom, Daddy' and 'I'm hungry, Daddy' and 'When are we going to get there?' and 'Tell me about New York, Daddy' along with 'Can we see the Statue of Liberty?' All of these questions were wearing thin on him.

"Doesn't she ever shut up, Mary? Doesn't she ever sleep? Look at how good, Tonia is. What's wrong with that kid? She was never that good."

He got tired of stopping and bought a can of coffee, poured the coffee out in the trash, and made Anna go pee-pee in the can. He got so impatient to get there, that he even hated to stop to empty the can out. So, it got pretty full.

"Dante, the coffee can is full again, we have to stop."

"My God, woman, quit giving that kid so much liquids."

"I'm just trying to keep her quiet."

"Here, hand me that can." Mary reached back and carefully handed Dante the can, wondering what he planned to do with it, but not saying a word against his impatience.

He rolled the window down and quickly peeled off the lid, tossing the contents out the window and into the void; a wind caught it and whipped it right back into his face. He sputtered and spat. Mary looked at him horrified, and started to laugh.

"What are you laughing at?" he demanded.

"I'm sorry, Dante. I can't help it, it's really funny." She was getting tears in her eyes, she could not stop laughing.

"Ha, ha, ha," said Dante.

"Stop the car, Dante!"

"Stop laughing and get me something to wipe my face off." Mary reached into the diaper bag and brought out two diapers, then proceeded to wipe and dab at his face.

"How appropriate, you give me diapers!" He laughed, too. He also pulled to the side of the road.

The rest of the trip was better, although Anna wasn't, and got popped a few times. Dante and Mary had a more relaxed attitude and made jokes about things. The incident with the coffee can had broken the ice and they had a slap-stick carefree attitude the rest of the way. They sang songs, 'Over the hill and through the woods to grandpa and grandma's house we go'. 'Jingle Bells, Jingle Bells,' Anna chimed in during the course. Then 'Down by the seaside sifting sand,' and Anna repeated,

"Down by the seaside pooping in the sand."

"What did that kid say?" Dante asked.

Mary reached over the back of the seat and popped Anna again. "I told you not to say that word." With a frown on her face Anna said.

"I'm sorry." She started screaming until she was blue.

They reached the outskirts of New York City in a snowstorm. Anna had never seen snow before and was excited. Mary had seen very little snow and was frightened to be driving in it. She asked Dante to slow down. Dante assured her they would be all right, and that he had been in snow all of his life. He pulled out to pass the car ahead of him and the car swerved out of control. Dante went with the swerve trying to get control of the car and the car spun around. Mary held the baby tightly and began screaming. Anna, instantly quiet now, fell out of the backseat and onto the floorboard. The car hit the shoulder and rolled over three times before coming to a rest in the ditch by the side of the road.

At Papa's house, everyone had been waiting eagerly for Mary and Dante's arrival. Dante had called and given them an estimated time of arrival the day before. The hours passed by the time they were to arrive. Mama and Papa grew extremely anxious.

"Where can they be? It's been hours, they couldn't be this late. I know something terrible has happened," Mama Vianney said, as she sat on the sofa wringing her hands. Papa tried to comfort her but was too worried to do any good.

"They'll be here, don't worry. What could have happened?"

"They could have been in an accident, that's what!" Mama answered angrily, speaking in Italian as most of the family did when they were with each other. Mama couldn't speak much English and the family always translated for her and conversed with her in Italian.

She had no other life outside of the home. The daily trip to the grocer on the corner, and since it was in an Italian neighborhood, spoke Italian to the ladies who shopped there. Most like Mama were from the old country and lived sheltered lives in their homes.

"I'm sorry. I do not mean to be short with you, but I cannot take this! Please find out what has happened. Dinner is almost ready and the rest of the family will be arriving soon. This snowstorm scares me and I will not be able to relax until everyone is home safely."

"It's not the first snowstorm we have had in New York, but I am worried, too. I will call the police and hospitals."

Dante was stunned. He seemed to have blacked out for a while. There was no way he could tell how long he had been unconscious. The baby was screaming in Mary's arms; Mary had not released her even though she was unconscious. Anna was crying softly and moaning. Dante looked over the seat and saw her on the floor between the seats. She seemed all right, but she had blood on her forehead. He took the baby from Mary's arms as she regained consciousness. Mary stirred and opened her eyes.

"Are you alright, Mary?"

"I think so, but my head hurts. The babies! Are the babies okay?"

"I don't know, I'm just now checking." He opened the blanket and looked Tonia over and couldn't find anything wrong with her.

"Let me have her. I'll quiet her down. Anna doesn't sound good."

"She seemed alright; I'll go in the back and see to her."

"Anna, are you alright?" he asked.

Anna opened her eyes and looked up into her father's eyes. "Daddy, you should have listened to Mommy and slowed down, I got hurt and hit my head!"

"I'm sorry, honey. It doesn't look serious. I guess it has been a while since I have driven in snow. I shouldn't have taken a chance."

"I'm really cold, Daddy."

It was starting to get really cold without the heater on in the car. Dante got back in the front seat and tried to start the engine but could not.

"I guess we have hurt the car, too. We will have to try and stay warm until someone comes to help."

He got extra clothes out of the suitcases in the trunk and everyone was wrapped warmly against the bitter cold.

"It's the best we can do for now. We just have to hope someone will come soon."

It was dark by now and the snow was still blowing fiercely. A couple of cars had passed them already, and had not noticed them on the side of the road, as they were further in the ditch and hard to see.

"Dante, we are going to freeze to death. I saw cars go by and no one is stopping. We need to go to the hospital and see if the children are alright. We can't tell by ourselves."

"The car lights are on, but I guess we are not visible from the road. I'll get the flashlight and go to the road and try to flag someone down."

Even with the flashlight Dante found it hard to see in the blowing snow. He was passed a couple of times before a woman in a car noticed him and told her husband; they stopped just past him. They both came back and helped the family back into their car and drove them to the hospital.

They were checked over and found to have only minor injuries, but were told they would have a lot of bruises. Anna was starting to get a welt on her eyebrow and a black eye to go with it. She had hit the crossbar in the front seat pretty hard. Dante had a cut on his rear that he could never figure out how he got. Mary had a couple of bumps forming on her head. The baby was unhurt. Luckily, she had a lot of blankets on her to protect her. Overall, they were very lucky and they knew it. They called the house and Papa answered the phone.

"Papa, it's me, Dante."

"Where the hell have you been? Your Mama and I are worried sick; we called the police and the hospitals. How can you do this to us?"

"Pop, we had an accident but we are all right."

"You had an accident? Oh Mary, Mother of God! We were afraid of that. What happened? Are you hurt? The babies? Mary?"

"Papa, I said we were all right, just minor cuts and bruises. I rolled the car and it was pretty scary but we were lucky."

"Thank God! Where are you? I'll send Vinnie to get you, you can't drive anymore."

"You're right, Pop, I can't drive anymore the car is ruined." He told them where they were and his brother picked them up and took them back to the house. There they were greeted with hugs and kisses and tears. Grandma soon gathered the two new grandbabies in her ample arms and cuddled them on the sofa.

All of Dante's family was there. All the Vianney's were talking in Italian and admiring each other's adorable children – where Anna and Tonia fit right in with all the dark hair and big brown eyes.

Mary had been introduced, and had received her fair share of attention but was now feeling left out. She had Tonia back and she was sleeping peacefully in her arms. Anna was running around with the boys who had taken to her immediately without any shyness. They were laughing and squealing and having a good time. Gloria noticed Mary sitting on the sofa alone and looking lonely, and went to her.

"They're quite a family, aren't they Mary?"

"Yes, they are. You can tell they are very close."

"Don't feel left out. We haven't seen Dante in three years. No one ever thought when he left that he wouldn't come back. He must really love you to be away from home this long." Dante's sister-in-law, Gloria, married to his younger brother, Antonio, had noticed Mary sitting alone with the baby and had gone to her to include her in the family.

"We had meant to come sooner but so much has happened," said Mary.

"I know. I'm sorry about your Dad."

"Thank you. It was a shock." Mary, now embarrassed, wondered if they knew anything about how her Daddy had died and began fiddling with the baby's blanket.

"You sure have beautiful girls," Gloria said, mercifully changing the touchy subject.

"Thank you. I was just noticing how much my girls look like part of the family; they are all handsome children and your Gina is a beautiful baby."

"Thanks. Come on, I'll show you where to put the baby to sleep, and you and I can go in the kitchen to help Grandma get the food on the table. I bet you all are starving? We have been nibbling while waiting for you to get here. Boy, we were worried. I sure am glad you are all right. I bet you are still shaken up."

Gloria offered to take the baby, and Mary now rising, did feel shaky. "Please, will you take her and lay her down. I am shakier that I thought."

"Maybe you should lie down awhile with the baby." I'll get you a glass of wine; I think you could use one."

Mary and Gloria were to become good friends; they had a lot in common being the only blonde-haired women in the room. Gloria and Antonio had been childhood sweethearts but, unlike Mary, Gloria was brought up in the Catholic Church. Their connection, being married into the family instead of being born into it, and they both had baby girls about the same age.

Mary took the glass of wine offered to her by Gloria, and began to relax. "I'll be all right now; I don't want to miss anything. This house is amazing and I do want to fit in."

"Oh, you will fit in all right. Those girls of yours made you an instant member of this loving family. Little Anna has taken to the boys, and we are going to have a hard time keeping them contained the rest of the evening."

The house was huge, three floors, and a basement, a bathroom and a kitchen on each floor, and on the second floor another living room. Each of the children had left the home to start their own families, and each in turn, had returned to live there when they had had bad times. Mama and Papa were always happy to welcome them back. The house was big and dark. The furniture was ornate and polished to a gleam. The sofas and chairs overstuffed, trimmed in dark wood and covered with heavy tapestry. Crystal chandeliers sparkled in the large foyer, where the winding staircase led to the second floor, and over the huge dining room table. Shaded lamps gave off a soft light. Mirrors with gold leaf trim and beautiful landscapes hung on the walls. The carpets on the shiny wooden floors were many and of rich colors. Family photos were everywhere, on top of the bureaus, on side tables, on the piano, and the fireplace mantel. The fire, crackling in the large marble fireplace over which hung the biggest mirror of all, and that mirror was now reflecting the family in the living room.

Two brothers with one's arm around the other's shoulder, talking softly, and Mary and the sister-in-law on the sofa watching the kids play. Mary was taking it all in. She had never seen a home like this; immaculately clean and shiny, and showing a certain old world charm and middle class elegance. The house was big and intimidating to Mary but she felt she could get used to it. It was like the family that lived there, and they could fill it up with their love and their beings. She knew they had not always had such nice things, in fact, Dante had told her of living in a tenement in the Bronx when he was a kid and how poor they were for a while. He told her how he and his brothers would share an apple and one would say, 'And I get the core?' But now this family fitted the surrounding and she wanted to be a part of it. 'Tomorrow, I will feel better and make a better impression on them.' She thought.

The next day being Christmas Eve, was festive from morning until evening. Grandma sat on the front porch in the morning and being very plump, was able to hold at least three grandchildren on her lap. She sat here every morning and fed the sparrows, which had come to know her and would come right up and eat out of her hand.

Anna and Tonia instantly loved the beautiful fat grandma who could whistle softly and birds would come to her, sit on her shoulder, and eat out of her hand. If anyone was watching, they would have instantly seen that Grandma didn't have to speak English to communicate her love to her grandchildren.

The Christmas tree, the biggest Mary had ever seen, was lit with candles and decorated with many shiny balls, tinsel and garlands. Under the tree was a mountain of presents. The children, after running around the house chasing each other, would soon sit and gaze at the presents and lights, until finally exhausted, lay down under the tree and napped. During nap time, Grandma Vianney would sit on the sun porch and listen to Italian Opera on the radio and doze in her chair for a while. The children were allowed one present to open before going to bed, and each picked the biggest one.

The next morning, all the children woke early, and went around the house waking everyone up and exclaiming 'It's Christmas. It's Christmas. Everybody get up. We have to open the presents now!' The parents and grandparents donned housecoats and descended the staircase to gather around the tree while Grandma fixed thick, rich coffee topped with cinnamon, for the parents, and coco, topped with whipped cream, for the children. By the end of the unwrapping of the gifts, the whole living room was covered with paper of many colors. Gloria and Mary tried to gather the paper while Dante started a fire in the fireplace. The paper was thrown in and a blaze arose that stunned everyone. They then took just a little at a time to add to the blaze. "Easy does it," said Papa, "No singed eyebrows today please."

After lunch, Grandpa Vianney and his boys went for a walk where they each were given a tiny cigar to smoke. Grandpa was allowed only two cigars a day – one he smoked while he walked the neighborhood after lunch, and the other he smoked in the evening when he would walk down to the corner Grocers. There were tables out front there, and they could get a cup of strong Italian coffee and the old men sat and smoked and talked of the days gone by.

Everyone seemed to get exactly what they wanted for Christmas: sweaters for the men and beautiful blouses and coats for the women, for the girls, all kinds of dolls, with toy trucks and cars for the boys. Each little face was beaming with the excitement and surprise as they tore into the packages.

The next day, Grandpa had a special surprise for Anna. They were going to the famous toy store, FAO Swartz, and get a special present she could pick out. Anna was spellbound, as the store alone was a gift. So many choices, things she had never even known existed. She strolled down the aisles and would grab something and say, "This one Grandpa." Then she would put it back and pick something else, and would repeat, "I want this one Grandpa Vianney." Finally, she saw exactly what she wanted. There on a shelf was the most beautiful doll she had ever seen. The doll seemed to shine alone on the shelf. "A bride doll, Grandpa, it's a bride doll!" She exclaimed. This was what she wanted. Grandpa reached up, and got the doll for the little girl, each with big grins on their faces.

"I think you have made a good choice. This doll looks just like your mother, with the blonde hair and all."

They would get three, one for each girl. Even though the other two granddaughters were too little to join Grandpa, he wanted to be fair and they would eventually be able to enjoy them.

Anna followed her Grandpa to the front of the store, now noticing more of the joys of the store; she tried to take it all in. She never wanted to forget this day with her Grandpa. In front of the store was a huge Santa Clause, automated to jingle his bell. All around was beautiful decorations everywhere and the shelves were crammed with every kind of toy imaginable. Anna, holding Grandpa's hand, gazed with wonder at everything.

Grandpa stopped at the counter and asked the pretty girl if she had any more bride dolls, as he told her,

"I have two more little granddaughters who need to have one of these dolls."

"You're lucky, we still have a few left."

Grandpa said they needed a dark haired one for Gina and a red haired one for Antoinette. The pretty salesgirl said she had a red haired one in the window but she would have to check for the dark haired one in the back, and she would be right back. They met at the counter. Anna held her doll tight in her arms. The salesgirl came with the two other dolls and rang up the bill. Grandpa handed the salesgirl the money and smiled at her. She smiled back, "That must be your Granddaughter, and of course you have a couple more, you are a lucky man."

"You don't have to tell me that." He beamed with pride as the girl admired the pretty little girl and the handsome and charming Grandpa.

Dante and Mary took the train back to California and everyone slept most of the way. At the train station, as they were leaving, there were many hugs and kisses and tears. Anna reached up for Grandpa's arms. He lifted her up, and she kissed his cheek and whispered in his ear, "Thank you Grandpa for my bride doll. I love you." He whispered in her ear, "I love you, too," and gave her a big hug.

Grandma bent down and hugged her granddaughter and said to her "Mi amore, bambina." Grandma's face was covered with tears now, as she fell into Dante's arms and gave him a kiss on each cheek and hugged him tight.

"Ma, you are going to squeeze the life out of me." He smiled at her and she smiled back.

"Mi amore," she said. Speaking in Italian, she begged him to come back soon.

As the train slowly left the station, the relatives followed throwing kisses at the family pressed against the windows waving and throwing kisses back.

"That was a wonderful trip," said Dante.

"Yes it was. I have never been anywhere so lovely and exciting," said Mary. She was wiping tears from her eyes. She had been embraced by the family and was touched deeply by their love, and would miss them as much as Dante.

PART FOUR:

HOME AGAIN

Chapter 13

CL and Mildred had their third baby. "It's a boy" was what was repeated to everyone present. A beautiful bouncing baby boy, so like his father, fair, blue eyes, and the two dimples. As soon as he could, his smile matched that of his father. He was named Dewey Cecil Eden II, but nobody called him that, he was Bubby from day one.

Now the family was overwhelmed, three babies just a year apart. CL worked the night shift at Lockheed and tried to sleep during the day. Almost an impossibility until the three babies went down for a nap, then he could sneak in a bit of sleep before going back to work.

It was chaos. All three still needing formula, diaper changes and attention. CL was expected to help as much as he could. They were adorable, all blonde hair and dimples, but as Diane displayed first and the rest would follow, each had a devilish and inquisitive nature. At the ages of three and a half, two and a half, and one and a half, they had the run of the apartment and were into everything they could get their hands on. One afternoon, while CL was trying to get a little nap on the couch, Bubby came in with a bucket of sand from the sandbox outside and dumped the whole bucket in CL's face. Mildred, who came walking into the room as CL sat up, sputtering sand from his mouth that had been open as he was snoring, broke out laughing.

"What are you laughing at?"

"Oh, I don't know, you just look so surprised. I told the kids to wake you for work and I think Bubby thought a bucket of sand would do the trick. I think he must have been thinking of water when he got the sand."

"It isn't funny," CL was wiping sand from his eyes and nose but couldn't help laughing too.

Mildred wanted to go on a trip to see her mother in Palmdale, just a little two hours away. They would stay overnight as her mother was not well and had not been to Glendale to see her grandchildren lately. Mildred had the bags packed and placed on the bed ready to go. She just had to run to the store to get some things for the trip. CL was supposed to watch the kids but had drifted off in his chair. When Mildred got home, CL woke up and Mildred asked him where the kids were. And he answered her,

"They were here a minute ago."

"Oh, my God, you were sleeping weren't you? Those three can't be out of sight for one minute."

She rushed through the apartment looking for the kids. She found them in the bathroom. The tub was full of water and lots of suds. And the three children were stirring the tub full of clothes with wooden spoons.

"What's going on in here?" she asked.

Diane and Sissy chimed in, "Look Mommy, were washing the clothes for the trip."

Each of the kids had big happy grins on their faces. Mildred said, "Oh No!!" And went in to the bedroom where she found the empty suitcases on the floor. The trip to Palmdale was put off for another time.

The pressure finally got to CL and the tropical fever came back. He had a bad time of it for awhile and had to quit his job. The family moved in with Ada and Earl, as they had plenty of room, and CL was still weak. Elephantitis is called such, because the symptoms can sometimes consist of swelling of the extremities, along with the fevers. It also affects the nervous system. Stress being one of the great factors of bringing on an attack. CL had not experienced any swelling and this was the first attack of the fever since he got back from the Navy.

Mildred got a job as a clerk, at the drugstore on the corner to help out, and Ada was left with most of the childcare. CL finally got his strength back, but had a hard time finding a job. He started to get depressed and then he started drinking. He would go out looking for a job and then stop at a bar, have some drinks, and then come home. He was a happy drunk, but Ada was appalled. She realized what CL was going through but her experience with drinking men was something she could not handle. She would say to him,

"CL, you know what drinking does to a man; don't you remember how your Daddy was?"

"Ah, Ma, I'm not like my Daddy, I'll find a job soon and everything will be alright. It just makes me feel a little better right now." Ada didn't believe it.

Anna came down with a cold that turned into bronchitis, and then asthma. First, just wheezing; and then there was hardly any breath at all. Mary took her to the doctor and he gave her some tests. Said she was allergic to something. The asthma and the bronchitis kept coming back, and the worst was when Mary found her turning blue from lack of breath. Anna was rushed to the hospital and was diagnosed with phenomena. She was kept for a week in the hospital and given more tests for allergies.

Anna was sick all the time, and experienced phenomena four times, and had to be hospitalized each time. Mary kept taking her to the doctor and the tests continued. Finally, she heard of a doctor that specialized in Asthma and took Anna to this doctor. After a few more tests, he came up with a list of things Anna was allergic to; suggesting they move to an area where it was known to be good for asthmatics. Anna was allergic to cow's milk and had to drink soy milk. She was allergic to fish, and chocolate, dust, and animal hair. Anna said she was allergic to peas too. "Peas make me sick too, mommy." The place they were advised to move to was Sunland, California.

After high school and before moving to California, Dante had gone to Business College and was a Certified Accountant. So after the war, he had quit his job at Lockheed and gotten a job with the State of California as a CPA, and was making enough money to make the move.

Sunland was a nice little town, just on the other side of the Foothills from Glendale, and at a higher and cleaner altitude. They bought a little house with a nice backyard. And Anna was a lot better, as long as she stuck to her diet, stayed away from animals, and Mary cleaned all the dust balls from under the bed.

Anna started Kindergarten in the fall. Mary dressed her in pretty little dresses and cute shoes. She stood her on the toilet seat to fix her hair every morning, always with bows to match her dresses. Anna was shy, and sometimes was teased for her dresses and bows. But Anna liked the way she looked in the mirror every morning, when Mary would say, "Now take a look at how pretty you look." So she kept the bows in her hair and ignored the other kids.

One morning she said maybe Mary shouldn't put the bows in her hair today. And Mary said,

"I thought you liked the bows?"

"I do, mommy, but the kids tease me."

"They do?"

"Yea"

"Well they are just jealous that you look pretty, and maybe their mothers don't care if their little girls look pretty or not."

So Anna wore the bow and tried to hold her head up and smile prettily; the kids stopped teasing her about the bows. But the boys wanted to see under her dresses, so they would chase her home trying to pull up her dress and see her panties. She was embarrassed about this but didn't tell her mother.

That year it snowed in Southern California. Mary and Dante had friends over for dinner and the snow stated to fall in the early evening. Everyone was staring out the window or going out to see the wonder of snow in California; letting the flakes land in their hair.

The friends left early, even though they all said the snow wouldn't last, but they better get home before the roads got slippery.

The next morning when everyone got up, Anna being the first, she had looked out the window and cried with excitement. "It really snowed last night, I mean it really snowed." She was squealing and jumping up and down and clapping her hands. Dante, Mary, and Tonia all gathered at the front window and stared at the sight with astonished wonder. It had snowed four feet overnight. No one could remember when this had happened before, or if it had been predicted last night.

It was a beautiful sight. Anna and Tonia were both jumping up and down now. "It's snowing in sunny California. It never snows in California." Repeating what they had heard their parents say many times.

"Can we go out?" They chimed together.

"Can we? Can we? Please, Mommy. Please, Daddy."

"Wait a minute, wait a minute," Dante said in control now.

"We have to check the weather report. I'll turn on the radio and see if I can get any information." First, as always, static, then adjusting, and then the weather man. . .

"Well, folks take a good look out your window this morning. This is a sight rarely, if ever, seen in Southern California. Four feet of snow on the ground, and still snowing in the foothills. Flakes falling as big as quarters were reported to the station this morning. As you can see, the roads are impassable and all schools will be closed. I am sure you won't be able to get your cars out of the drive way, anyway. I doubt anyone of you own a snow shovel. I was told at some of the higher elevations there are a few rusty snow plows. But the advisory is to stay off the roads. But it sure is a beautiful sight."

"Can we go out? Can we go out?" "Pleaseeeeeeeeese?" again from Anna and Tonia, staring at them with pleading smiles on their little faces, with their hands folded in front as if praying,

"Ok," Mary said. "I'll get your rubbers and coats, and you will have to have mittens, and a hat." She went to get the cold weather gear and came back and dressed the anxious girls. They were let out the front door and saw other kids playing on the street making snow balls and giggling.

Mary called the school just in case. The operator answered and said that a few children and teachers had shown up, they were inside the auditorium, and that a magician was coming to entertain them in a little while; but school would not be held as usual.

Mary called Anna to the door and told her that there was going to be a magician at school in the auditorium, and if she wanted to go, she should ask Daddy to take her. Anna said she was happy to play with the neighbor kids, and ran off squealing. She fell on her butt, got up, and tromped in the snow up to her knees.

Anna soon got bored with the neighborhood kids and her mittens were soaked. She went to the door. "Mommy, my mittens are all wet." Mary heard her but had no more mittens, then she remembered the heavy wool socks that Dante had carried from New York and were still in his sock drawer. She went to get them and found two pairs. 'One for Anna, and one for Tonia, whose mittens, must be wet too.' She thought. She went to the door where Anna was waiting and she helped her put on the socks.

"Socks?" Anna said, her nose was wrinkled up as she looked over the gray wooly socks.

"Do I have to wear socks on my hands?"

"They are perfect. See how they go all the way up and you won't get snow in them."

"Ok, I am going to go to the school. Daddy doesn't have to take me." Anna was looking for a response from Mary but she was looking over her head for Tonia.

"Tonia, come here and get rid of those wet mittens."

As soon as Mary had shut the door, she went back into the kitchen where she could see the kids through the window. She was cooking breakfast and chocolate chip cookies at the same time. She now bent down to check on the cookies. And she didn't see Anna leave the yard. When she looked out the window she didn't notice that Anna wasn't there, she was too distracted because her first batch of cookies had stuck to the pan, and she was scraping them off of the cookie sheet.

Anna had started her walk to school. She had done this every day the past few months, but today was different. She noticed how pretty everything was and stopped to look up into the trees. They looked beautiful, the sun was out, and the tress sparkled and dappled with the rays bouncing off the snow laden branches. Her feet were slow going; every step took effort to pull her foot out of the snow. But soon she found a path where other children had trampled the snow, and now she was skipping along fine as ever.

She arrived at the school and went directly to the auditorium. She left her rubbers where everyone else had left theirs and was going down the isle when she was stopped by a teacher.

"Anna Vianney, can I see your note?"

"What note?"

"All the kids here today had to have a permission note or be with their parents."

"No note." Anna said.

"Okay, you go down and sit with the other kids and I'll be right back." The teacher was going to go to the office and call Anna's parents.

At home, Dante had gone out to get the soggy paper and saw Tonia but no Anna. He went back in the house and asked Mary where Anna was. She said Anna was playing with the other kids. She had, just a few minutes ago, come for dry socks.

"I didn't see her outside."

Mary was instantly put on alert. "You didn't see her?"

"No, I didn't see her." Dante voice was rising with panic. "Come on, let's go look for her."

They went out the front door and each called for Anna. Then they asked Tonia where her sister was.

"I don't know, Mommy; she was over there a minute ago." Both parents being outside didn't hear the phone ring in the kitchen.

"We have to search the neighborhood; she couldn't have gone far in this snow." Both Mary and Dante combed the street up and down calling for her.

Mary was crying by now and Dante was getting extremely anxious.

"Why weren't you watching her? Anybody could have picked her up."

"Don't say that Dante."

"I'm going in and call the police." A child being kidnapped is something every parent will always fear.

As Dante entered the house the phone rang again. It was the school and the teacher told him that Anna was in the auditorium with the other children, and the reason she was calling was that Anna didn't have a permission note to be there.

"If you give me your permission, she can stay here for the afternoon."

"Oh, I don't think so; I'll be there soon and get her." He slammed down the phone and it fell to the floor; he picked it up and went to get his heavy overcoat.

Mary had just come into the house; she was ringing her hands and crying.

"Did you call the police?"

"Don't need to, that little stinker of ours went off to the school."

"She went by herself?"

"I guess so, she is there now. I am going to go get her, and when I do, she is getting the spanking of her life."

Dante entered the auditorium, went directly to Anna and picked her up by the collar. He cradled her in his arms and picked up her rubbers from the line of galoshes that were by the door.

He plunked her down in the car. "What's the matter, Daddy?" Anna was gazing up at Dante with a puzzled look on her face. Dante then relented and hugged her tightly, and kissed the head covered with curls, her forehead and cheeks.

"We thought you were lost. Why didn't you tell us you were going to go to school?"

"I told Mommy."

"You told Mommy? She didn't know where you were."

"I told Mommy I was going to school."

"You were not to leave the yard without permission. You are never to leave the yard without permission."

"I know, but I told Mommy."

"Did she say you could go?"

"Well, I told her I was going."

Anna's punishment was that she had to stay in the bedroom all the rest of the day until dinnertime. She cried herself to sleep. The last thought she had before going to sleep was. 'It isn't fair. I told Mommy I was going, and all the kids will trample my snow in the front yard. My snow, the only snow I will ever have.'

Chapter 14

CL couldn't find a job and his drinking was getting worse. Ada was sick, 'Not again, not again, oh God please don't let CL go down that road like his Daddy did.' Every Sunday they would all go to the Baptist Church that was on the corner of the next block. Then they had an elaborate dinner prepared by the women at Ada's and Earl's house. It was seemingly a perfect family gathering, but CL would sneak into the bedroom where he had hidden away a bottle of whisky and take a couple of swigs. No one knew except Ada, and she hid the fact just as CL did.

Anna was crazy about CL, he was so handsome, and when all the little kids were down for a nap, he would always take her for a walk and spend time with her. She was the oldest of all the kids and this time alone with her Uncle Dewey made her feel special. Any other time all the little kids would be crawling all over him.

CL had reoccurring bouts with the fevers and would spend days in bed sleeping. Ada would sometimes hear him moaning in his sleep, then he would scream and sit straight up. Ada would be there in a second and ask him if he was alright. He said he was, just tired and had had a bad dream. Ada knew something was terribly wrong and asked him if he wanted to talk about anything. He said he was just upset because his health wasn't good and he couldn't get a job.

Well, he did get better and he found a job, but it was a job at a gas station and he had to work nights.

By this time, Dante was ready to find a bigger house for his family. He found a house, well a garage, on a big lot right off Foothills Boulevard on Scoville Ave. He saw the potential; the lot was zoned for multiple dwellings. There was Foothills Boulevard, just one house, and then the big lot with the garage. From the lot you could see the backs of the shops that faced the boulevard. He found the owner in the house next door on the left. Mr. Farmer owned the lot and the one next to it with his house on it.

He let Dante into the garage, which wasn't bad; it had a kitchen and a bathroom. Besides just being a garage. Mr. Farmer said his oldest son had stayed there for a few years, and had added the kitchen and bathroom. Dante made a deal with Mr. Farmer and then he went to get Mary.

"Mary, it has potential."

"What potential? It's a garage!"

"You'll see, I'll fix it up. I have it all figured out."
And he went on to explain how he could make the house
great. They could sleep in the garage while he put a
living room on the front, and then he would raise the
roof to make the attic into a bedroom for the girls. Mary
had resigned, for she knew the deal was done and she
would have to just go along with it.

So they rented out the tiny house on Matthews
St. and moved into the garage on Scoville Ave. The
garage became the bedroom. It was large enough for
Mary and Dante's bed, and bunk beds for the girls.
Dante started right away building the front room. The
kitchen was large, as it ran the length of the garage, but
he was going to add a porch to make up the difference
where the front room would jut out. They slept in the
bedroom with the garage door still on, while Dante
worked on the front room.

Sunland was a nice little town, and being just up
the street from the main part of town was fun for Anna.
The best part of the town was the park. Sunland Park
was like no other park ever planned for a town. It had a
skating rink, a small amusement park, and a big swimming
pool, besides just being a park.

Mary began to enjoy living close to town, Scoville
ran right to the center of town, where the only stop light
was. On the corner was a dress shop, where she would
gaze at the fashions that changed with every season.
Next to the dress shop was a bakery. Every morning the
smells of baking bread and pastries would waif from the
back of the bakery to the house. Everyone would wake
hungry from the smells of the bread baking.

She would put the girls in a stroller and walk down to the town, then across the street to the diner that was there to have a cup of coffee. Then she would go to the grocery store next to the diner and get the groceries she needed for the day.

Of course, she was always stopped by someone who wanted to admire the two little girls.

The town had an Easter Parade every Easter and events at the park every holiday. Anna and Tonia made friends with the two little girls that lived next door. And the patio that was on their property had a sidewalk that led to the circular driveway that fronted the house next door.

Mr. Farmer had owned all the three properties at one time, and the main house on the right of Dante's garage was now divided into apartments. The two girls lived in the tiny apartment, and an older couple with a little shy boy lived in the front apartment.

Anna, Tonia, and Carol and Tessa, the two girls next door, would skate all afternoon; around and around the patio, then down the sidewalk, and around the circle driveway and back to the patio. They made up all kinds of scenarios where they were famous skaters and they would dress up in some of Mary's old clothes, scarves, and hats. They would be the happiest little girls playing all afternoon under the big pine trees that dotted the two lots.

One of the things Anna liked best was to climb the pine trees. She was very agile, and would go up to the top on this one tree and stay for hours picking off the bark. Then she would climb a little higher and make the tree swing back and forth.

Mary, coming out one day to witness this activity had a fit.

"Anna, you come down here right now." Anna looked down at her mother and saw the angry look in her eyes. Mary looked up and saw the scared look in Anna's eyes.

"Anna," she said softly, "Just come down slowly, one branch at a time."

"Are you going to spank me?"

"No, honey. I won't spank you; just come down slowly and be very careful." Anna did as she was told and then spent the rest of the day in her bed. She was never to go up that tree again, which was the last thing Mary said to her before she left her.

Anna didn't go up that tree again, but there was another one she hadn't climbed before; this tree's branches were too high off the ground for her to reach. So she got her tricycle, got up on the seat, and caught the lowest branch, as her bike rolled away from under her feet and across the patio.

'Oh, no,' she thought, 'how will I get down?' Well, while she was up there she was going to make the best of it. But this tree had more bark and harder bark; she was getting scratches and a lot of sap on herself. She decided she better not climb this tree anymore and started shouting for Mary.

Mary looked out the window and saw the predicament Anna was in and went out to investigate.

"I see you got yourself in a fine mess this time." How in the world did you get up there?" Anna pointed to the tricycle. Mary couldn't help smiling, but before she turned back to face Anna, she put a stern look on her face. "Well, I just think you will have to stay up there for a while, I told you not to climb trees, didn't I.?"

"No, Mommy, you said not to climb that other tree anymore." Mary was already walking back into the house.

Anna was left in the tree for a long time. She kept calling for Mary but Mary wouldn't relent. She knew she was safe enough. She had seen how Anna had her arms wrapped around the tree trunk. She watched her from the kitchen window as Anna went thru her tantrum.

"Mommy, Mommmmmmmmmmmy, Oh Mommmmmmmmmmy, my hands hurrrrrrrrrt, Mommy." Then she would be quiet for a while, then it would start again. Then she remembered something from church. "Jesus, Jesussssssssssssue, help me."

After some time of Anna taking her punishment, a man came onto the driveway. Anna perked up.

"Hi Mister, who are you?" The man looked up into the tree and saw Anna there.

"What are you doing up in that tree?"

"Well, it's like this, I got my tricycle over there," she pointed to the tricycle and the man looked at it and knew what was next. "I got on the seat and climbed up here, but the tricycle decided to roll over there and now I can't get down. Would you help me?" So Anna found a way out of the tree and she did learn her lesson about climbing trees. But that night, she heard Mary and Dante whispering about the way Anna had manipulated the salesman to get her out of the tree, and they both laughed. And Anna smiled, as she fell to sleep.

Chapter 15

Mary made friends with Agnes, the mother of Carol and Tessa, They had coffee together and Agnes invited Mary to go to her church with her. Mary said she always went to the Baptist Church in Glendale with her mother. And Agnes said they were having a revival meeting and a visiting pastor was going to be there all week, and they could go any night. Mary said she would think about it. Agnes said he did healing too, and this interested Mary.

Anna had had more bouts with the asthma; the sawdust from Dante's building project was making her sick.

Mary told Agnes that she wanted to go with her the next night. Dante wouldn't go but Mary, Anna and

Tonia, and the neighbors all went together. The church was the Four Square Pentecostal Church. Mary had heard about, and the people who had told her about it said the churchgoers were fanatical. But as soon as the service began, Mary knew she was in a different kind of church than she had been attending with Ada. She liked it.

She felt the spirit of the Lord in this church, much different from the quiet sever services of the Baptist Church. This was more like the Southern Baptist Church she had attended when she was a child in Texas.

The church was an old church, but this only added to the atmosphere of the Holy Churches in the larger cities Mary had visited. All of the arched windows were stained glass, presenting Jesus and God in their benevolence, Jesus with the Children, Jesus with the Lamb, God in Heaven surrounded by angels, and Jesus ascending thru the clouds into heaven. The pews were dark cherry wood. Behind the pulpit on the stage, and behind the choir stands, hung heavy red velvet drapes; that Mary would find out sometime later on, concealed the Baptismal pool.

The choir came in wearing gleaming white robes trimmed with gold around the v-neck, the sleeves, and the hem. It was quite a sight against the red of the drapes. They sang the gospel hymens that Mary remembered singing in the old church back home, the ones Ada had sang around the house. Then the pastor said an opening prayer, and introduced the evangelist that was there for the revival. He gave a stirring sermon, and his voice rose, and his hand went up in praise of the Lord. He preached of past sins and the ever present mercy of a loving God and how Jesus had died on the cross for our sins. And all we had to do was ask for forgiveness and he would forgive us, and we could walk in peace with God. He said that when our time here on earth was over, we would go to be with Jesus, who had gone before us to prepare a place for us.

He asked for all of the people to bow their heads and pray this prayer of forgiveness, and ask the lord to forgive them and come into their hearts. Then he asked for all who had prayed that prayer to come to the front of the church and kneel at the altar before the living God.

By this time, Mary was crying, as this is what had been missing in her life. She had gone through her life with the heavy burden of sin, and had never really prayed this prayer before. She had missed the personal relationship with God and the nearness she now felt. She rose from her seat, Anna and Tonia followed her to the front of the church. They kneeled down at the altar as so many others were, and Mary held Anna's hand while Anna held Tonia's hand. The organ music was playing softly, a song Mary remembered, Jesus is Calling, Come Home, Come Home, all who are weary come home, come home... The evangelist was passing behind each prayer, and touching them each on the head as they were receiving Jesus into their hearts and souls.

Mary was still crying, and Anna was now crying while Tonia was in shock; she was just too young to understand. The Holy Spirit descended and filled the church. Mary felt it as chills filled her body.

As the organ was playing the beautiful old song, the evangelist went back to the pulpit. He thanked Jesus and praised him for the souls he had received into himself this evening. Praise to our God, Hallelujah, Thank you, Jesus. Then he asked if there was anyone there that needed healing, and if they would form a line and he would pray for them.

Still with tears running down her face, and still holding Anna's and Tonia's hand, Mary got in the line for healing prayer for Anna. She saw miracles happen before her, and when she reached the evangelist, he asked her if she believed that Jesus could heal. Mary answered that yes, she did. He asked her what was the healing that she needed and she said, "My daughter, her name is Anna; she has suffered from Asthma and bouts with Phenomena for six years." Mary presented Anna to the evangelist. He put his hands on both sides of her little head, asked Jesus to have mercy and heal this little girl from this aliment and for it to never come back again. Mary was praying also, as were all the people with their voices raised to the Lord. The evangelist asked Anna if she believed the Lord had healed her and she answered, "Oh, yes, I do." Then he said for her to thank Jesus and she said, "Thank you, Jesus." Then he asked Mary if her faith was as strong as the little girls, and Mary said she did believe the Lord had healed her daughter.

When they arrived home, Dante asked,

"How did it go?"

"Oh, Dante, it was wonderful." Dante could see that Mary was shinning with a new kind of joy.

"Tell me about it."

"Well, best of all, Anna was healed of her Asthma, but before that happened, we received the Lord as our Savior. That was probably the best part, because if we didn't believe in Jesus, Anna wouldn't have been healed."

"Really?" Dante said with skepticism in his voice.

"Yes, it really happened."

"Well, I can see you are convinced, but one visit to a new church doesn't convince me."

"You'll see," said Mary, as she left Dante in the living room and went to put the girls to bed.

Anna lay in the upper bunk of the beds and was overcome with joy. She started singing softly. 'I've got Joy, Joy, Joy down in my heart, down in my heart. And I will never be sick again.'

The next morning, Anna got up and ran into the kitchen, where Mary was preparing breakfast and told her mother,

"Mommy, I want hot chocolate for breakfast with the real milk." Mary looked surprised, but considered the implications and knew if she didn't comply it would shake the faith of the little girl, voiding the new faith she had acquired.

Anna had her hot chocolate. It was to her, like the best thing she had ever had. Then for lunch, Mary made her a tuna sandwich. While eating her lunch, Anna said she wanted a puppy. Mary thought 'Dear Jesus, thank you, you have made us a regular family again.' Then she said to Anna,

"Anna, we will have to talk to Daddy about that." She paused, thinking of how Dante had shown no real understanding of what had happened to his family.

But Anna ate and asked for all the foods she had been denied for the many years she had been ill. She didn't get sick, and Mary thanked God every day for the healing.

The years of Anna's sickness had been hard on the whole family. The trips to the hospital, the terrible bouts of Phenomena; when they didn't know if Anna would survive or not. And Dante noticed the happiness that had come over Mary, and Anna was happy too.

But it took some time before Dante would attend church with the family. It was the Sunday they were going to do baptisms and Mary, Anna, and Tonia were going to be baptized. Mary had been baptized in a river in Texas when she was a girl, but she wanted to do it again in her renewed faith. Ada and Earl were to come, and they would have dinner at the Vianney's house after church.

The church was as always; beginning with the choir singing, the pastor gave a short sermon about how John the Baptist had baptized Jesus in the river at Jesus' request, and how we perform baptisms to signify our cleansing of sin. Then the red curtains were opened and a pool was exposed. The wall behind the pool had a scene painted on it of Jesus being baptized by John, and light shown all around the pool. Each, in white robes, one at a time, descended into the water, the pastor who was already standing in the water with a white robe on, took each new Christian; held the back of their head and with his other hand lightly pushed the Christians under the water.

He said, "Child of the almighty God, I now baptize you in the name of the Father, the Son, and the Holy Ghost. Go and sin no more." The choir had parted, and now stood on each side of the opening and were singing softly, "At Calvary, Mercy there was great and grace was free, pardon there was multiplied for me, there my burden soul found liberty, at Calvary." At this, Ada was crying, the spirit came over her, and she quietly received the blessings of forgiveness, salvation and release from the quilt that she had lived with for so many years.

Dante was touched as well, and started attending church with his family every Sunday. They would still go over the hill, through Shadow Hills to Glendale, to have dinner with the rest of the family at Ada and Earl's house.

Ada was happy again. She played Christian music all day and went around singing the hymns again as she had done before; a beautiful sound to anyone who was there to hear it.

Mary played the Christian music, too, where she had played the country music before, and the house was filled with love and joy.

Chapter 16

Mary was pregnant again; Anna being ten years old and Tonia eight years old. This pregnancy was unplanned, but welcomed as Dante still wanted a son. CL and Mildred, and their three children, were still living at Ada's house. The money each of them was making now did not allow for rent to be paid. So Ada took care of the three precious little grandchildren and loved them to death. They were a handful but they were CL's children and in her eyes they could do no wrong. When they shook out baby powder and Ivory snow all over the living room; Ada had come in to find the mess, they chimed in one voice,

"Grandma, isn't it beautiful? It snowed in here." She held her breath for a few seconds, considering giving each one a good paddling. Then she said,

"It doesn't snow in Southern California. Now who is going to clean up this mess?"

The three grandchildren looked at Ada with huge eyes and expressions that said, 'I guess you are.'

"I guess I will have to clean this up since you are too little to vacuum, but this wasn't a good thing you did. You will each have to go to your room for a nap now, until your Daddy gets home."

"We are really sorry Grandma," said Diane; being the oldest and now the most ashamed to have given the wonderful Grandma more work to do. She took the two others to their room and told them to stay right there until Daddy came home.

CL had been promoted to the day shift, as he had shown his ability to work on cars, but this just gave him more time for drinking. A couple of nights during the week, he would stagger in late, and especially Friday night, they could count on him being late and drunk. CL was depressed. He wanted to provide for his family, and he didn't feel well all the time. He drank more. He got into fights in bars and once was arrested for drunk and disorderly conduct. Everyone, except Mildred, tried to hide the fact that CL's behavior was out of control.

"Now Mildred, Ada would say, "You know he is sensitive about the war and all, he just needs time."

"But he is drunk most of the time."

"No, he's not; you're making a mountain out of molehills. He works hard at the gas station, and as soon as things get better, I am sure he will find a better job.

Then you can move into your own apartment." Ada loved having the family with her, but Ada sometimes, just didn't like Mildred.

"What else can he do? He's just a grease monkey."

"Mildred, I show you respect because you are his wife and the mother of my grandchildren, but I will not hear you talk about my son like that. He will be alright, he is smarter than you think." 'You fat cow,' Ada thought. Mildred had put on weight, and Ada didn't approve.

Ada had always been brought up to look as nice as she could, and take care of herself, and Mildred had let herself go. But when Ada had these thoughts about Mildred, she would always ask God to forgive her for her thoughts. She prayed every night on her knees that CL would get better in his health, that he would stop drinking, and that he would get a better job. She begged God to help him, to save him. Some nights were long; CL didn't come home until very late and then would stagger into bed. Ada was awake and praying all the time, until she heard him come in and his door shut, and she knew he was safe.

After the war, good jobs were hard to come by. Thousands of men were coming home from the war. The factories that were making artillery and parts for planes and everything they needed for the war were shut down. So families' living together was common in these times. "You'll see, Mildred, CL is a good man. He'll come out of it, as soon as he finds a better job."

But he didn't find a better job. His drinking, depression, and stress caused him to lose faith in himself. And the words of his Daddy came back to him, 'You're nothing but a worthless little piece of dirt. You think because your mama and your sister adore you that you will make it in the real world. All you can do is work on cars; you don't have a brain cell in your empty head.'

The war, what he had been through, the friends he had made and lost, the killing, the maiming, the conditions he had to endure, these things he couldn't talk about to his family, even now. But they haunted his dreams at night. He would hear the pop of gunfire and the screams. The crying of the other men at night haunted him the most, because he never cried, not once, during the whole war. His hard daddy had scared the cry out of him. He wasn't brave during the time he spent in the war, for he was just as scared as the rest of the men, but he knew he had to go on and endure if he was ever to go home again. So he gritted his teeth at night, squeezed his eyes shut, wrapped the pillow or whatever he had around his head, and kept in all the feelings he was experiencing.

He trained himself to think of home, Ada, Mary, and their faces, their smiles, and the kisses and hugs they always gave him. He wrapped himself in these thoughts and was sometimes able to get a few hours sleep, only to wake the next morning and realize he was still on the disgusting island. The Japanese were waiting for him to get up, and it would all start over again.

Mary worried about CL. She prayed for him, too. She had begged him to come to church with her. Every week at Sunday dinner, she noticed that he was getting thinner and his always bright eyes were dull. Instead of the big grin he always had for them, he only was able to give a weak side smile that was almost like a smirk. His answer when asked if he would attend church was, "I go with Ada sometimes to the Baptist church, but I don't think I can go with you Mary."

'But why?' she would ask.

'I can see your enthusiasm for this new church, but I am just not ready for that kind of church yet.'

His faith in God, after what he had been through, was shaky. Yes, he had called out to God and prayed many nights, but the horrors of war leave a man wondering if there is even a God up there. If he is seeing all this destruction and massacre, why wasn't he doing anything about it? Sometimes he thought.

'Even if I make it out of here alive, the ghosts of the other men who I have seen slaughtered will haunt me the rest of my life.' And he would feel like-What's the use- but he had to go on, he had to endure. If for no other reason than to show his Daddy that he was worth something.

Mary and Ada had agreed not to tell CL about his Daddy's death until he was safely home. And when they did, he just took it as if it didn't mean much to him. He was numb to the effects of death.

He took his joy in his children and in Mary's children. He played with them and held them; this was the only time Mary and Ada saw the old CL. Tears would come to their eyes as they watched him laugh and play with the kids.

He would let them climb all over him and they all adored him. Each time, when Mary would first see him, she would hug him close to her, afraid to let him go. And then she would hold his face in her hands and study his face. Then she would kiss his forehead and they would hug again. They knew he was not doing well. They knew it was a big adjustment for him to come home and start all over again. Unfortunately, the darkest parts of his thoughts were never known to them.

Chapter 17

CL knew the way he was acting was upsetting the whole family, so he resigned to do better. He had been changed to the day shift about six months ago, but now he thought he should go back on the night shift, so he wouldn't have the time to go to the bars. At the bars drinking with other men like him, who were everywhere, and some without jobs and complaining of the war; sometimes he felt better and sometimes he got more depressed. He would think 'Here are men who understand what I went through' and the telling of the war stories was some kind of release. But in the end, by the next morning, the way he felt and the guilt, would just add to the depression he was having.

So he started working nights and he quit drinking. He put on a good face for the women and children. He tried to be the happy go lucky guy he was at one time. But he still had the night terrors. And when he woke up each day, it got harder and harder to put on this happy face for everyone else.

One night, he had been sitting at the desk in the office. Hardly anyone had come by that night and he started thinking again of what a failure he was, and how he was disappointing his family. There was a liquor store next door to the gas station. He walked over there and bought a bottle of whisky. He took it back to the office and started drinking. The more he drank, the more the thoughts came flooding back to him. His Daddy's words especially. He thought, 'I guess you were right, Daddy. I am just no good. Why did I end up like this. Everyone thought I was the golden boy with the big smile, except for Daddy, of course. I am glad he is dead. After what I have been through, if he had ever touched me or my mother again I know I could have killed him myself.'

He was very tired now and it was closing time. He locked the office door that led to the pumps, and went into the garage part of the gas station where his car was parked. He got into the car and turned on the engine. He remembered that he hadn't lifted the garage door. But he sat there thinking, 'Everyone would be better off without me.' Then he thought about how much he loved his children and how much Ada and Mary would be sad if he was not there. He started to get out of the car to open the garage door. But he sat back down. He was so tired. There was a blanket in the back seat, he reached over the seat and got the blanket. He wrapped himself in the blanket and lay down on the front seat. He started to drop off but woke himself up. 'Oh God, Oh God, I am so tired, please forgive me.' Then he drifted off; the last thing he saw in his mind was the faces of the three little children he was leaving behind and he started, and tried to wake up but it was too late, the dark pulled him under.

The next morning, Ada and Earl were having coffee in the little cozy kitchen and something gripped Ada's heart. She looked at Earl; he looked back at her and saw fear in her eyes.

"Did you hear CL come home last night?" She asked him, her voice shaky.

"No, I didn't, did you?"

"No, I didn't either." Ada started visibly shaking.

Then there was a knock on the door. Earl said he would get it, and for Ada to stay right where she was. "Who would be knocking on our door at this time in the morning?" he said, as he got up to answer the door. "Don't you move from that chair until I get back."

He was afraid now that it was bad news. Since CL had quit drinking and seemed happier, everyone had relaxed a little, and now he just knew it was going to be the worst kind of news.

He opened the door. Two men in suits were standing on the porch. Earl went through the door and met them on the porch.

"Mr. Dagon?" asked the first one.

"Yes, what are you here for?"

"My name is Detective Rogers and this is Detective Patton. Do you have a son named Dewey Cecil Eden?" Earl went pale.

"Yes, well, he is my stepson."

"Is Mrs. Dagon here?"

"Yes, but why don't you just tell me what this is about, she is not feeling too good right now."

"I am sorry to hear that, and I am sorry to tell you the news I have brought to you this morning." He paused, as this was the worse part of his job. "Well, this morning, when the owner of the gas station where Mr. Eden worked came in, he found the doors were locked and your son's car was parked in the garage. The engine had been running for hours, until it ran out of gas and he was found dead, Carbon Dioxide poisoning."

Earl had backed up to the door by now and was weak in the knees.

"CL is dead?" he gasped.

"Yes, Mr. Dagon. He passed away some time during the night. CL is that what you called him?"

"Yes. Oh my God, how can I tell his mother?"

"I am very sorry for your loss, Mr. Dagon. Do you want us to come in and tell her what has happened?"

"No, I mean, yes, I can't do it, this will kill her; he was her baby."

"I know what you mean," said the kind detective. "Listen, we will come into the house and you can introduce us and you must call a doctor and, do you have a local pastor who can come over?"

"Yes, we are regulars at the church right on the corner."

"OK, let's go on in then."

Ada had left the kitchen and was sitting on the sun porch couch where she could see and hear a little of what was being said on the porch. She had a good idea what it was all about. But she was sitting straight with her hands folded on her lap when the three men entered the foyer, and saw her sitting in the sunroom.

"I'm over here now, Earl. I hope you didn't expect me to stay plastered on that chair in the kitchen all this time, did you?"

"Ada, there are men here to talk to you."

"I know who they are," she looked angrily at the two men. "What do you men want with us here this morning, knocking on the front door at six o'clock in the morning?"

"Mrs. Dagon, I have asked your husband to call the doctor and the pastor for you."

"I don't need anybody, where is my son?"

"I am sorry to tell you this, but he is at the coroner's office right now."

Ada got up off of the couch and ran at the detective and started pounding on his chest. "Don't tell me that; you liar!"

The detective grabbed her hands as she sunk to the floor. He picked her up, and as he saw Earl at the phone, he asked where the bedroom was and told him he should call any close family members right away.

The detective carried Ada into the bedroom. Earl said the doctor would be there in a few minutes. The detectives took Ada into the bedroom and laid her on the bed. She looked at them and then started screaming, "You liars! You liars!" She flayed her arms, she tried to hit the detective again, and then she just screamed a blood curdling scream and fainted.

The detectives stayed until after the doctor had gotten there. They said someone would have to identify the body soon, as they left.

Earl was sitting by the bed when the doctor came in, and Ada woke up. "Why is the doctor here?" Then she remembered; she had overheard what the detectives were saying to Earl on the porch. They said CL was dead. She looked up at Earl and asked him,

"Is CL dead?

"Yes, I am afraid that is what they said." Ada started shaking again, and tears seemed to spurt out of her eyes. "Where's Mary? Get Mary, I need Mary!" She was hysterical by now, and the doctor gave her a shot to calm her down. She drifted off into a hazy sleep; tears still falling over her cheeks.

Earl now knew that the next thing he had to do was just as bad as what had already happened. He called Mary's house and luckily Dante answered the phone. Earl explained what the detective had told him and Dante was shocked but remained calm.

Mary was sitting at the kitchen table not six feet from him. He turned his back to her in case he was showing any sign of what was going on. He had already decided not to tell her what had happened until they were at Ada's house.

Earl had said the doctor and pastor were there. Dante was worried about more than Mary's reaction to this sad news. She was now seven months pregnant, and this would have to be handled very carefully.

"Who was that?" Mary asked.

"It was Earl, your mother is not feeling well and he wants us to go over there and see her."

"Is it serious?"

"I don't know. The doctor is with her and they want us there right now."

"Okay, I'll get my coat; I hope it's not something serious." Mary had a worried frown on her face. Dante didn't say anything. In the car, Mary again said she hoped it wasn't something serious, and Dante didn't say anything. She looked at him and knew it was something serious, but she had no idea what it was. She sat in silence until they reached the house.

Chapter 18

Mary and Dante arrived at the house as Mildred and the kids were getting up. Their room was at the back of the house and somehow, the commotion hadn't disturbed them before now. Earl heard them in the kitchen as Dante and Mary were coming into the living room. Having forethought; he called the neighbor across the street to come and get the kids, while heading off Mildred in the kitchen.

Dante lead Mary to the living couch, where he crouched down in front of her and took her hands. He quietly explained what had happened, She keep saying "No, No, No," to anything he told her. She had started crying. She bent her head and covered her face with her hands. Dante gave her a tissue, and she held it to her nose. She had realized the importance of keeping the conversation at a low level by the way Dante was talking so softly.

"Where is my mother?"

"She has been given something to calm her and she is resting now."

"I have to see her."

"She wants to see you, too."

Mary was shaking all over, and crying softly. Dante helped her up and lead her to her mother's bedside.

Ada felt Mary's presence and opened her eyes; they were puffy and red rimmed. Ada had a stricken look on her face, but when she saw Mary and Dante she opened her arms, and Mary crawled into bed with her mother. Ada moved over to accommodate Mary's ever increasing size. The two women held each other, and now they were able to let out all their emotions.

"CL is dead," Ada said.

"I know, Mama."

"But how could this happen?"

"Dante is calling the police station to get a full report, but is seems he went to sleep in his car and the motor was running." Mary answered her, she was trying to be calm for her mother's sake, but her voice was shaky. Tears were running down the side of her face as she was turned to face her mother.

"That doesn't make since, are they sure it is CL?" Ada was crying continuously, a gasping kind of sob that shook her body.

"Well, he had identification, and that lead them to us, someone will have to identify him."

"Oh My God, I can't believe this. Oh God, in Heaven, don't let it be CL, there has to be a mistake."

"He didn't come home and the body was found in his car. I don't think, Mama, that there was a mistake." Mary held her mother now and each woman sobbed and cried in each other's arms. Dante had gone and got the doctor to come in and stay with the two women.

Earl was in the kitchen with Mildred and the kids. Mildred was serving them breakfast. And she turned to Earl and asked,

"Where is CL? He didn't come home this morning. Why are Mary and Dante here?"

The three little pajama clad children looked up at Earl at these questions, as if they sensed something was the matter. Their cereal spoons held in mid air.

Earl was at a loss about what to do. Dante was in the kitchen area sitting in an alcove that was there, with a desk that the phone was on. He had just finished his calls and came into the main kitchen.

"Mildred, can we go into your bedroom? Something has happened and I would rather not say anything in front of the kids."

"Okay, you're scaring me, Dante." He put his arm around her shoulder and led her back into her bedroom. She was shaking already. He asked her to sit down on the bed. About the same as he had told Mary about CL, he told Mildred. She started screaming right away.

"Are you crazy? He'll be here any minute."

"Not this time, Mildred; I'm afraid, not this time."

The children hearing their mother in anguish had come to the door of the bedroom and were staring at Dante and Mildred, their eyes as big as saucers. Just then, the neighbor lady, Angelina, from across the street, entered into the kitchen and saw the three little children standing at the door of the bedroom. Mildred saw them too, and screamed,

"My babies, what's going to happen to me and my babies?" At that, Angelina carefully took the children out of the doorway and into the living room. She told them that their mother wasn't feeling well, and they were going to go over to her house for a while. Each one looked up at her and said,

"What's wrong with Mommy and where is Daddy?"

Angelina looked at their beautiful faces and she had tears in her eyes. "We will be alright in a little while. You just have to come home with me for now." She knew in her heart that nothing would ever be right in this family ever again. So she took the three little children over to her house for the time being.

The doctor came into the bedroom where Mildred was and he gave her a sedative to calm her, because she was hysterical by now. She kept trying to get out of bed and kept asking, "Where is CL? Where are my babies?" All the men knew the sedatives would wear off and the house would be chaos. These strong women would be stricken as they never were before in all their lives.

Dante had called Agnes from Earl's and asked her to go over and help out with Anna and Tonia. He said that he would be back in the evening.

Well that day was horrible. The doctor was worried about Mary because of the pregnancy, and when she came out of the bedroom where she had been comforting Ada, she collapsed on the floor of the dining room. She was then taken into another bedroom and put to bed. The doctor could only give her a small amount of sedative because of the pregnancy. But Dante stayed with her through the rest of the morning. The pastor was with Ada, and Earl was with Mildred.

Finally, in the late afternoon, everyone gathered in the living room except Ada who was too weak to get out of bed. They asked questions of Dante, who had talked to the police station and the detectives. He tried to explain what had happened. He told them that CL had closed up for the night at the gas station and was preparing to come home. He had gotten in his car, turned on the engine, but he had forgotten about the garage door. It appears he might have just wanted to get warm because he had a blanket wrapped around himself. It was a very cold night. Anyway, he fell asleep and the Carbon Dioxide poisoned him.

Nothing was said by Dante about suicide to the family, but the police had their suspensions about the circumstances. They had found the bottle of whiskey that was almost empty. They had asked Dante if CL had had emotional problems. And Dante had said he guessed that he did have some problems. So an autopsy was to be done as soon as someone could go to the morgue and identify the body. Dante and Earl were the ones who would do that, the first thing the next morning, as there was no way any of the women could do it.

Everyone sat or walked around the room in a daze for the rest of the evening. Then food started arriving from the neighbors. And the children were brought home. Mary tried to explain to them that their daddy would not be home for a while. The rest would have to come at a later time, as Mary was having a hard time accepting that she would never see her little brother ever again.

Ada stayed in bed and Pastor Mike, as he was called, sat with her. She wailed against God, then asked the pastor to forgive her. She asked him why or how could God take away the most precious thing in the world to her? And how was she to survive without him? And his children, how are they going to go on without him? Ada knew about death, but it had never hurt like this before. The pastor tried to answer her questions. He took his Bible and opened it, and then he said to her,

"I know. I have heard these questions from mothers before, and these are the hardest questions to answer; the one thing I am sure of is that; you will have to have the most faith you have ever had. You need God right now and you have to believe that he didn't want your son to die; he doesn't want you to suffer.

But Ada, we don't have all the answers, I don't have all the answers, I only know God wants you to trust him, believe in him, and to lean on him at this time. Only by doing this, will you come through it." Pastor Mike turned to Romans 4:20-25 and read from the Bible.

> *'He staggered not at the promise of God through unbelief; but was strong in faith, giving glory to God.' 21-And being fully, persuaded that, what he had promised, he was able also to perform. 22-And therefore it was imputed to him; 23-Now it was not written for his sake alone, that it was imputed to him: 24-But for us also, to who it shall be imputed, if we believe on him that raised up Jesus our Lord from the dead: 25-Who was delivered for our offences, and was raised again for our justification.'*

He explained that Paul was talking about Abraham who was given a son in his old age, but that the promise held, was there for us too. So you can be sure that God has your son in his arms right now, and is giving him the comfort he did not receive here on earth.

"But, pastor, I loved him so much, I prayed for him so much. Was it my fault? It was my fault! I couldn't give him what he needed. It was the war; it could have been the war?"

"Ada, there are many things that can contribute to this kind of thing happening, but from what I know of you and your family, you cannot take blame for any of this."

"I divorced his father. His father committed suicide because of me."

"Ada, Ada, we all make mistakes and we work through them with the love of God. I know you, Ada, you are a good and loving woman, I don't know a kinder woman, and you are always giving to others. I don't believe any of this is your fault." He continued,

"It is common, when this kind of thing happens, especially to a young person, for everybody to try to take the blame or to blame others. But your son was a grown man, and God gives us free will to do what we want. Sometimes we do not make the right decisions and something goes terribly wrong. That's not your fault or Gods fault. God sent his Son to die for our sins, so that when we die we have the most wonderful place to go; here we will experience the perfect love of God that we will never find here."

Ada said, "Thank you, Pastor Mike. I do understand more now, but I know I am going to be sad for a long time."

"I understand that, too, God gave us these feelings and it will take time. You will miss your son, but you will eventually feel better."

"Maybe, but I know. I will never be the same."

"Ada, just keep praying for God to be with you; he will help you find the strength to get through this."

"Pastor Mike, could you hand me my Bible over there on the bureau, I need it now. And I want to be alone, except for Mary. Could you tell her to come in here."

"Of course, I will."

Dante went home to be with Anna and Tonia; he told them about their Uncle Dewey, and they both cried. Their Uncle Dewey had been their favorite. His tall handsomeness and good humor had always made him special to them. "He's in Heaven?" they both asked.

Mary stayed with Ada that night, neither one of them leaving the bedroom. Mildred was in her room with her three little ones. And Earl slept in the quest room.

Mary and Ada spent most of the night crying, praying, and talking about Little Dewey. They had reverted back to the name they had called him when he was little. They recalled things about him that were special. Mary had asked Ada what she had talked about with the pastor, and Ada repeated word for word what Pastor Mike had told her.

And Mary said, "It all sounds right, what he said, but it doesn't help right now."

"I know," said Ada. And they took comfort in each other, and finally did sleep a little.

Chapter 19

Mary and Ada both woke with a start, upon looking at each other, they both started crying again. They allowed their selves a little time of quiet grieving, and then they got up and started preparing for the day. Ada said, "I have been thinking about Mildred and the kids; I don't want them to leave. I need them here with me." Ada was thinking of the resemblance of Bubby to CL when he was little, and how each time she looked at him he smiled just like Little Dewey had.

Dante arrived. He had arranged for Agnes to help with the girls for one more day. Mary embraced him. He asked how she was doing, and she said that she was doing as well as expected. Ada came in and started to prepare a breakfast. The three little ones came running into the kitchen as soon as they heard the rattle of dishes.

"Is Daddy here, has he come home yet?" Ada's hand went to her mouth and tears began to run down her face. Each one of the children looked to Ada for an answer. She took a tissue from her pocket and sat each one of them down at the kitchen table in their regular spots. Then she called Mary to please come in to the kitchen. With Mary there for backup, Ada sat down with the children and told them that their Daddy went to be with God.

Diane said, "In Heaven?"

And Ada said, "Yes, honey. Your Daddy is in Heaven with Jesus and God."

Sissy said, "Okay, but when is he coming home?"

Diane looked at her sister and she said, "Heaven means he is not coming home." Her voice rose as she said these words. All three of the children started crying and got up and ran back to the bedroom where Mildred was still sleeping. They jumped in bed with her and cried, "Where is Daddy? Grandma said he's in Heaven, and he's not coming back."

Mildred hugged each one of them and said, "I'm sorry, but yes, that is what happened. He had an accident and Jesus took him to Heaven."

"I want my Daddy," each one repeated. They didn't understand. They had heard of Heaven but not in a permanent way, and this seemed like a permanent situation.

"Will we ever see him again?" Diane asked. Mildred barely able to keep herself together, and not a strong believer of anything Christian, but she was ready to give the children the stock answer that seemed to help.

"Yes. There will be a day when we will all go to Heaven and we will be with Daddy again."

"Okay," they all said, as they crawled under the covers with their mother. Bubby and Sissy with their thumbs in their mouths sniffling, and Diane hugging her mother and crying softly. Diane being the oldest had some understanding of what lay ahead for the three little kids.

Eventually, Mildred made her way into the kitchen with the children in tow. The first thing she asked Ada was, "What's going to happen to us now?"

Ada answered her, "Well, I want y'all to stay here with me."

"But that's not right."

"It's the rightist thing I can think of right now. I know we don't see eye to eye about everything all the time, but we need each other right now."

Ada opened her arms to Mildred and Mildred melted into them. The three little kids grabbed them around the legs and they stood that way for a few moments; they each seemed to understand each other.

So it was settled. Mildred, who had thought she would have to quit her job and go live with her mother in Palmdale, was going to stay with Ada and Earl in their big, comfortable house. She supposed that now she would be accepted by Ada; fully as part of the family.

She had always known that Ada kept a shield up against her because she came between her baby boy and Ada. She had always thought of CL as a Mama's boy, and now the shield had come down.

The next two days, Ada kept busy, planning for the funeral, and the reception at the house for after the funeral. This kind of thing was what she did best, and it helped her to keep busy. Mary kept saying, "Mama, aren't you overdoing it a bit." Then Ada would collapse, crying into Mary's arms. Then she would pull herself back together and start right back in preparing the house for what was to come.

The autopsy was done and the death of Dewey Cecil Eden was proclaimed by the coroner as an accidental death by Carbon Dioxide Poisoning. And the funeral was to be held the next day.

The service was held at the Baptist Church where they had all attended at one time, and it was filled to capacity. Ada was popular among the parishioners and the neighborhood and everyone came. The service was a beautiful service; there were many flowers and Ada had requested 'At Calvary' to be played on the organ, as this had become her favorite song now.

The church had a private section where the family sat, to the side of the main chapel, where during a regular service the choir sat. This was an extra addition, not usual in most churches, but made for a place where the family could express their sorrow without everyone witnessing it.

But the crying was heard by the parishioners and there were not many dry eyes in the church that morning. The limousines took CL to Forest Lawn where the grave site service was held. Then, just the closest friends and family came back to the house where there was all kinds of dishes of food provided by the neighbors.

The expense had already been taken care of. The year before, Ada and Earl had bought plots in Forest Lawn and paid for their funeral arrangements. They never imagined that one of their own families would be put in one of these graves before them. They never saw fit to purchase another grave.

Life continued on after that. Mourning continued on. The homes of Mary and Ada were quieter than usual, until the morning Mary went into labor.

"Baby Boy?"

"Yes, Father."

"It's time to go?"

"Is it really time to go?"

"Yes, it is time to go."

"But Father, I don't want to go. I love it here, it's wonderful."

"I know Baby Boy, but there are those who need you now, and it is your time."

"I knew my time would come, but is seems too soon. I will miss you and Jesus and all the angels."

"My Son, I will always be with you,"

"You will?"

"Oh Yes. You have a lot to do and a lot to learn. I will be with you always. If you ever need me, just call my name and I will be there."

"But Father, what if I forget to call on you?"

"You don't have to worry about that, I will remind you."

"And what if I forget again?"

"I will remind you a thousand times if you need me too."

"How long will I be gone?"

"It won't be long at all, it may seem like a long time but it is just a very short time."

"Okay Father, I will go. You always knew I would go, didn't you?"

"Yes, my son, I always knew. Try not to forget how much I love you; you are very special to me."

"It's part of the plan isn't it, Father?"

"Yes son, it is part of the plan."

"I love you, Father."

"I will always love you too, Son."

"I love you father, I love you, I love you, I love you."

Darkness, and then light.

WAHHHHHHHHHH. "It's a boy," the nurse said, as the doctor spanked the baby on the backside and he wailed. "A healthy, baby boy, ten toes and ten fingers, and a head of black hair," said the doctor.

The doctor placed the baby on Mary's stomach as he cut and tied the cord. She glanced at the baby and started to cry. The doctor asked her if those were tears of joy and Mary said they were. Then the doctor said, "It is always a miracle of life to me every time I deliver a baby. It never changes. Babies are a gift from Heaven." The doctor gave the baby to the nurse to clean up, and then back to Mary who couldn't take her eyes off the beautiful baby boy.

They named the baby, Stephen Joseph Vianney, and as so happened it was the very day Stephen Joseph was born that the head stone was being laid on Dewey Cecil Eden's grave at Forest Lawn. The inscription read:

HERE LIES THE BODY OF DEWEY CECIL EDEN, HIS SOUL IS IN HEAVEN WITH HIS HEAVENLY FATHER. HE WAS OUR BELOVED SON, FATHER AND BROTHER. HE WILL LIVE IN OUR HEARTS FOREVER. Born June 25, 1924; Died February 13, 1954

Dewey Cecil was 29 years old when he passed away, nobody knew if he had meant to commit suicide or if it was an accident. Ada and Earl had gone to the gravesite before coming to the hospital, they didn't tell Mary about the headstone that day.

Mary was back in her room and holding the baby, showing him off to Dante when Ada and Earl came into the room. They had flowers and balloons. And Earl had cigars.

"We don't smoke, Earl," Mary said.

He said, "They're chocolate." And little laughs were had.

Ada approached the bed. Mary looked up at her, "Can I hold the baby, Mary?" Mary got a lump in her throat as she handed the baby to Ada. Ada sat down on the side of the bed with Mary.

She gazed into the eyes of the pretty baby boy; she stroked his cheek and touched his hair. Mary was watching her and tears came to her eyes. Ada turned to look at Mary and saw the tears in her eyes, and she started crying too. Then something passed between the two mothers.

Something like infinity and the circle of life, and a secret they would each hold in their hearts.

AUTHOR'S NOTES

The stories told here are true events, fictionalized, that either I was there for as the character Maryanna, that I was personally told, or heard while my mother and grandmother talked at the kitchen table when they thought I was too young to understand. Are there more stories? Of course there are – in God's worlds there are infinite possibilities.

Silvia Petretti was born in Glendale, California. She had three children and now has five grandchildren. For 15 years, she made her home in Sedona, Arizona, and then moved to Phoenix, Arizona where she now resides.

The first book Silvia Petretti published was a story about her third child Mark, who passed away in 2009. The book is entitled *Mark N. Greene, My James Dean*. *The Glass Pedestal* was written many years ago after the death of her mother and never published until now.

Silvia Petretti worked in Real Estate and is now retired and spends her time writing, doing art projects, and gardening. She attends Phoenix First Assembly of God and is a partner with Joyce Meyer's Ministries.